Dorran's life could be better.

He likes his job as a freelance translator, and he loves his boy-friend, but he and Eli have been fighting, and he's not sure how to solve their problems. There's nothing Dorran can do about seeing ghosts, no matter how much Eli hates it, and the situation with Eli's family isn't helping matters. Dorran wants to give Eli time to deal with his parents, but he also doesn't want to be kept a secret.

Dorran temporarily forgets all about his problems when his neighbor, Emanuel, wakes him up at one in the morning and thrusts a bloody knife in his hands. Emanuel insists he didn't kill his boyfriend. Dorran believes him, but everything points to him. Dorran isn't sure he'll be able to prove Emanuel had nothing to do with the murder, not even with the help of Francis, the ghost who shares his apartment. He's going to try—there's no way he'd letting an innocent man go to jail when he might be able to help, even though that might be the last drop that ends his relationship with Eli.

Leverage
Copyright © 2019 Catherine Lievens
ISBN: 978-1-4874-2606-4
Cover art by Angela Waters

Published by eXtasy Books Inc or
Devine Destinies, an imprint of eXtasy Books Inc

Look for us online at:
www.eXtasybooks.com or www.devinedestinies.com

LEVERAGE
LOST IN TRANSLATION BOOK 3

BY

CATHERINE LIEVENS

Leverage: in translation, the practice of reusing translated terms in new translations or the rank which evaluates how much of the previous translation can be used.

CHAPTER ONE

Dorran was enjoying himself until Eli's phone rang.

He sighed and paused the movie. He was used to having their lives interrupted by Eli's phone. With his job, Eli was often called away from him at any given time during the day, and while Dorran wished he wasn't, he'd never said anything about it. He'd known what he was getting into when he'd started dating Eli. You didn't date a detective without having to share him with his job.

Eli snatched the phone from the coffee table, looked at the screen, and grimaced. That was enough for Dorran to realize it wasn't work. Eli *loved* his job, even though there were dead bodies involved.

"Hey, Ma," Eli said. He wasn't looking at Dorran, which was just as well.

Dorran was never happy when Eli talked to his mother or any other member of his family.

Dorran had liked the Hayes back when he and Eli were best friends as teenagers. He'd liked them when he and Eli had realized they were in love.

He didn't quite like them now that they were still trying to get Eli to date women even though he'd come out to them.

Of course, he didn't know that for sure, because he hadn't seen them since he and Eli had gotten back together. Eli made sure the Dorran part of his life and the family part were kept separated, as if he was afraid that his family would find out he and Dorran were together.

He probably was.

"Yeah, I'll be there for Sunday lunch, don't worry. Unless something comes up with work."

Dorran could almost hear Eli's mother. The woman's voice was loud even when she didn't try to be. He still remembered that, and it would have made him smile if he hadn't been so miffed.

He knew he should get up and give Eli privacy. Eli kept sneaking glances at him as he talked to his mother, no doubt to gauge his reaction. But Dorran stayed where he was, his arms crossed over his chest, his gaze firmly on the paused film on the TV screen. This was one thing he wasn't going to make easier for Eli—brushing him off as if he didn't matter, as if he wasn't even in Eli's life.

"No, Ma. Yeah. I'll be alone." Eli glanced at Dorran again.

Dorran didn't move. Of course Eli would go alone to Sunday lunch with his parents. He and Dorran had been back together for months now, but he still hadn't told them about him. They didn't know he spent half his nights in Dorran's bed. They didn't know he spent most of his evenings on Dorran's couch, making out with him.

"No, Ma. I told you, I'll be alone. You know I don't . . . no, I don't have a girlfriend. Come on, Ma. Why are you even asking that? You know I'm not seeing anyone right now."

Why was she asking that indeed?

Dorran decided he'd had enough of listening to a one-sided conversation in which Eli's mother tried to fix him up with one of her friends' daughters. It happened often enough that he knew about it, and he hated that Eli didn't just remind his mother that since he was gay, he wouldn't do much with a woman in his bed.

Eli never did, though.

Dorran got up and went to the kitchen. He could still hear Eli's muttered conversation with his mother, but at least he couldn't see the expression on Eli's face. It was always a mix of embarrassment, pain, and defiance, as if he expected Dorran to force him to tell his mother about him. Dorran wished he could sometimes, but he knew better than to try. Eli would tell his mother about him when he was ready to do it and not one second before that.

But would he ever be ready?

Dorran realized it was hard for Eli. Even though he'd come out to his family several years ago, they hadn't accepted it. They still behaved as if he was just a bachelor who hadn't yet found the right woman. It had to hurt to see the people who meant the most to you behave that way.

But there was a reason why Dorran had broken up with Eli when they were eighteen, and this was it. He hadn't wanted to stay in the closet, and even though he'd loved Eli back then, that had been more important than love.

It still was. Eli hadn't asked Dorran to hide their relationship. Hell, he'd even told his partner on the force about them. But when it came to his family, he'd isolated Dorran from them, and Dorran was starting to be hurt by that. He didn't want to become another son to them, but he also didn't want to avoid them for the rest of his life — or as long as his relationship with Eli would last. They were a huge part of Eli's life, and Dorran thought he was, too. Keeping them separate was stupid, and hurtful, at least to Dorran.

The fridge opened on its own, and a bottle of water came floating out of it. Dorran smiled and took it before it could land on the counter. "Thanks, Francis."

An invisible hand squeezed Dorran's shoulder.

He didn't know if Francis was becoming stronger as more time passed since he'd died, or if Dorran's ability to see and feel him was. Not that it mattered. Dorran was glad he had Francis right now, even though Francis was a ghost. "Thanks," he said.

Francis wasn't visible right now, but it took him a lot of

energy to do that, so Dorran wasn't worried. Francis tapped the back of Dorran's hand in what Dorran thought was probably a question.

He sighed. "It's nothing. I'm just tired of this situation." Francis tapped again. Dorran wasn't sure what to tell him. "I know Eli is trying to do the best thing for everyone, but I don't think the best thing for his family is the best thing for me, and I'm not sure where that leaves us."

"Dorran?" Eli called from the living room.

Dorran didn't have the time to get back there because Eli walked in. He forced himself to smile and opened the bottle of water. "Yes?"

Eli peered around. "Who were you talking to?"

He knew who Dorran had been talking to. "Francis."

Eli's expression twisted. "I hate when you do that."

"And I hate when you tell your mother that you don't have anyone in your life, but hey, you still do it. I guess we both have to deal with shit we don't like."

Eli's expression flattened. "It's not the same thing."

"You're right, it's not. I'm talking to a ghost. You're hiding our relationship from your family."

Eli rubbed his face. "I'm not hiding our relationship."

"Didn't your mother just ask you if you had a girlfriend?"

"She always asks me that. You know it."

"You're right, I do. And didn't you say you don't have anyone in your life right now?"

"Dorran—"

"No. You know what? If me talking to Francis bothers you so much, you know where the door is. It's not like I'm your boyfriend anyway, is it? You don't have anyone in your life." Dorran knew they should talk about it. He knew he shouldn't lash out.

But he had, and he didn't care. He wanted Eli to leave. He wanted Eli to admit they were together and to stop hiding him.

"Come on, Dorran. Don't be this way."

Dorran crossed his arms over his chest. "Are you *ever* going to tell your family about me?"

"You know it's complicated."

"That's what I thought. Goodbye, Eli."

"Dorran—"

Dorran shook his head and walked past Eli. He didn't want to listen to the same excuses Eli always gave him. He knew them by heart by now. He hoped Eli would leave. He didn't want to fight with him. He didn't want to say things he'd regret. No matter how angry this situation made him, he loved Eli, and he wanted to be with him. Eli was worth a lot.

But was he worth going back into the closet, even if only part-time?

Chapter Two

Dorran locked his door after checking that he had everything he needed to go to the grocery store—his phone, his wallet, the reusable bags to carry the groceries. He wasn't looking forward to this, but he was out of bread and milk, and pretty much everything else. Even the toilet paper was getting low, and that wasn't something Dorran ever wanted to be without.

"Hey, Dorran."

Dorran didn't groan, but it was a close thing. Instead, he plastered a smile on his face and turned toward Emanuel. "Hi."

Emanuel always looked gorgeous—and he always made Dorran feel like a troll crawling out of his nest. His long brown hair was tied back from his face, and there was a hint of stumble on his cheeks. Instead of looking unkept like Dorran would if he didn't shave every morning, Emanuel looked like he'd just rolled out of bed after a night spent making love to another gorgeous man.

"Where are you going?" Emanuel asked.

Dorran held up his bags. "I need food."

Emanuel laughed. "Don't we all. Hey, is everything okay? I heard you and your boyfriend fight last night."

Dorran sighed. Of course Emanuel had heard them. He lived next door to Dorran, and while the apartments were somewhat soundproof, they could still hear what was happening if someone was yelling. Dorran and Eli hadn't exactly been screaming, but Dorran had been especially loud, and Eli had slammed the door when he'd left. "We're fine." He hoped Emanuel wouldn't push for more answers.

"You're sure? I know we're not exactly friends, but if you need someone to talk to or a shoulder to cry on . . ."

Dorran blinked. Emanuel was right — they weren't friends. They saw each other fairly often, but that was mostly because they lived next to each other, and the only reason Dorran knew what he knew about Emanuel was that he'd suspected Emanuel had killed the man Dorran had found when he'd first moved into his apartment. "I'm okay." He appreciated Emanuel's offer, but he didn't think he could tell him what was happening with Eli.

Emanuel nodded. "How about a coffee?"

"Right now?"

"Why not? I'm sure the grocery store will still be open when you're done."

Dorran wanted to say no, but he didn't want to be rude. He had to live next to Emanuel after all, and he should probably maintain their relationship — if he could call it that — at least pleasant. "Sure. Why not?"

Emanuel's smile was beaming. "Come on in, then."

Dorran had expected them to go to the nearest coffee shop, but he couldn't back out of this now. He followed Emanuel into his apartment. The smell of fresh paint slapped Dorran in the face, and he relaxed. He might not be an artist — he could barely draw stick figures — but something about the smell of paint always made him feel better.

Dorran stayed in the living room area to look at the paintings and sculpture there while Emanuel went to the kitchen to get the coffee ready. Dorran couldn't see him where he was, but he could hear him. He wandered along the paintings, leaning closer to a few of them to get a better look.

"Want another one?" Emanuel asked.

Dorran shook his head. "No. I still feel guilty that you

7

gifted me with the first one."

"It wasn't much. I'm not famous or anything."

Maybe he wasn't, but Dorran liked art, and he could tell when something was expensive. Of course, Emanuel had made sure to tell him he didn't need the money because his father paid his rent and whatnot, but that didn't mean Dorran felt better about it.

"Why don't you come to sit down at the table?" Emanuel asked, disappearing into the kitchen again. "Milk? Sugar?" he called out.

"Both, thank you." Dorran settled at the table and looked out the window. The sun was shining, and it felt like a betrayal, given how dark Dorran's emotions felt.

He was still angry. He also wanted to talk to Eli, to make him see that he couldn't do anything about seeing ghosts and that he didn't want to be kept a secret, not from the most important people in Eli's life. But he knew that if he tried to bring it up, Eli would probably get angry. Eli hated that Dorran could see and communicate with ghosts, and he hated talking about his family and the way they behaved about him being gay even more. Either of those topics would become arguments, and Dorran had enough of those right now.

Emanuel placed a steaming mug in front of Dorran. "There you go." He put down the milk and sugar next to the mug, then went back into the kitchen, no doubt to grab his own coffee.

"Thank you." Dorran still wasn't sure what the two of them were doing—trying to become friends? He wouldn't mind that. He didn't have a lot of friends. He worked from home, alone, and while he still had his best friend, he didn't see Charlie often enough since he'd moved out of the apartment they'd shared.

He should probably try to make small-talk or something. "I see work is going well," he started, but he wasn't sure how to finish that.

Emanuel slid into the chair in front of Dorran. "It's going, yes. Better than I thought. I've been selling a lot of stuff on my website."

"That's good." What else could Dorran ask about? He didn't want to give Emanuel time to think about the fight he'd heard last night. "So the job is going well. What about a boyfriend? I don't think I've seen anyone around lately."

Emanuel took a sip of coffee and shrugged. "I *have* a boyfriend. Well, kind of."

"Kind of?" Dorran leaned back in his chair. "What does that mean?"

Emanuel waved. "It's nothing serious. I mean, I like him well enough I guess, but he comes with a lot of baggage I'm not sure I can deal with. It's not like I'm in love with him or anything, and I don't think I ever will be. He's nice to spend time with, though."

That didn't sound like Emanuel was in love, no. Dorran wasn't sure how that kind of relationship worked—he'd rather be alone than be with someone he didn't think he could love.

Emanuel leaned forward. "But enough about me. I have nothing interesting to talk about anyway. What's going on between you and the cop?"

Dorran couldn't help but smile. It looked like Emanuel still held some resentment about Eli suspecting he'd killed John Mitchell. "The *cop* has a name, and he's a detective."

"Same thing. What's going on between you and *Eli*? It's not like you to fight."

Dorran sighed. He traced the tip of his finger along the rim of the mug. He and Emanuel weren't friends, but would it be so bad to tell him what was going on? Dorran no doubt needed all the help he could get. "He hasn't told his family about me yet."

Emanuel frowned. "He's not out to them?"

"He is, or at least that's what he told me. But from what I know, they're happily ignoring the fact that he's gay, especially his mother. She keeps pushing women toward him, and while he hasn't dated any of them, he also hasn't told his family that he's with me. When his mother asks if he's dating, he says no."

"And that hurts you."

"Yeah." Dorran looked at his coffee. "I get why he's doing it, but I can't help how it makes me feel."

"I understand that. Your family doesn't have a problem with you being gay, right?"

"No." His mother cared about nothing but getting drunk. Bettany, Dorran's sister, had never cared, and even Dorran's brother had come around.

"Can I give you some advice?"

Dorran smiled. "I guess."

"I understand where you're coming from, but also where *Eli* is coming from. You know I'm not out to my father, right?"

"You told me."

"Sometimes, family can be hard to deal with. They should be the ones who support you the most, but it doesn't happen often enough. Eli knows his family better than you do. You should talk to him and tell him how much it hurts you, but I wouldn't push him if I were you. That kind of thing never ends well."

"I'm not pushing." Dorran could have demanded Eli be honest, but he hadn't.

"Good. So no pushing, but don't let Eli walk all over you, either. What the two of you have is worth fighting for, but not if you end up hurting all the time. Think about what you want and what you can stand. Then tell him. It's obvious you can't go on like this forever."

Dorran knew that, but sometimes it felt like Eli didn't, like he'd happily keep Dorran a secret from his family for the rest of his life.

"You know, I don't mind watching movies with you, but it's kind of weird that you're half-transparent," Dorran told Francis without looking at him.

Looking would have made him freak out a bit. They were both on the couch watching some movie Dorran had put on. He hadn't picked something he knew he'd like, because he wasn't paying attention to it. Francis seemed to be, though. He'd settled next to Dorran earlier, scaring a year off him when he'd suddenly appeared there. Dorran wasn't sure if he liked Francis better when he was invisible or when he could look through him, like right now. He was glad not to be alone, though.

Francis' hand appeared in front of Dorran's face. He flipped Dorran off.

Dorran laughed. "That's what you use your ability to be visible for? To flip me off?"

Francis couldn't talk, or at least Dorran couldn't hear him when he tried to. He probably could if he focused and meditated, but he wasn't in the mood, especially not to have to hear Francis tell him to fuck off.

Francis rolled his eyes. Dorran was tempted to flip him off, too, but a knock on the door interrupted him. He and Francis looked at each other. Francis cocked his head, and Dorran knew him well enough to know he was silently asking who it was.

"I have no idea. I'm not expecting anyone. Maybe it's Emanuel. You know we had coffee earlier." It was weird, but Dorran had gotten used to sharing his apartment with a ghost, and he often talked to Francis when he was there. He'd told him about Emanuel when he'd come back from grocery shopping, and Francis had looked happy that Dorran was making friends with him. He'd known Emanuel when he'd been alive, and from what Dorran knew, they'd been friendly.

Eli? Francis mouthed.

Dorran wasn't sure if he wanted the person at the door to be Eli or not. "I don't know." He got up. "Just stay here, yeah? That way you can disappear if it's someone who shouldn't know about you." The only person who would be comfortable with finding Francis on the couch watching TV was Carole, but then, she was a psychic. She wouldn't have a reason to be here tonight, though. They hadn't planned to meet, and while they were friendly, they weren't friends yet.

Dorran opened the door. He wasn't sure how he felt when he saw Eli standing there. He'd wanted it to be Eli, yet he hadn't.

He crossed his arms over his chest and leaned against the doorframe. "Eli. What are you doing here?"

Eli rubbed the back of his neck. "Can we talk?"

This was what Dorran had wanted to do last night, but he was wary. "It depends."

Eli sighed. "Look, Dorran, I know how you're feeling. You don't like that I haven't told my family about you yet, and I get it. I wouldn't be happy if you were hiding me from the people in your life. But it's complicated."

Of course it was. Wasn't it always?

Dorran stepped aside to let Eli in. He didn't want to fight. He wanted to get into bed and cuddle, to enjoy Eli's presence while he could. Dorran had no way to know if Eli was going to stick around or if he'd want him to.

He'd been happy when they'd gotten back together, and he loved Eli, but this felt too much like what they'd had years ago when Dorran had broken up with Eli because Eli didn't want to come out.

Eli walked in. "Thank you."

"What for?"

"For giving me a chance to explain."

"There's nothing to explain, Eli. You won't tell your family about me. You're letting your mother thrust women at you even though you're gay."

"I don't want to push them. You don't know how hard things were when I told Mom I was gay. She didn't speak to me for weeks, Dorran. I don't want that to happen again."

Dorran knew he couldn't understand what Eli had gone through. He'd never been close to his mother, and his father had died when he was a kid. He didn't have the kind of relationship Eli had with his family with anyone. He wasn't even close to his siblings, even though he saw them more often after what had happened to Chris, his brother.

So maybe he didn't understand. "Are you going to keep me a secret from them forever?"

Eli raked a hand through his hair. He looked like his day hadn't been easy — his tie was loose, his shirt rumpled, and there was a stain of what Dorran thought was coffee on the bottom of it. "I *want* to tell them about you. I want them to know I'm happy and in love. Can you give me more time?"

Dorran nodded, even though he wasn't sure he could. He didn't want this conversation to be the end of their relationship, though, and he knew that was what would happen if he said no. "How long, Eli?" he forced himself to ask.

"I don't know. I'm going to be firmer when it comes to the women Mom keeps introducing to me, okay? And I'll tell her I don't want to date any of them."

Dorran supposed it was something. He wanted more, but maybe — hopefully — this was the first step Eli would take.

It wasn't like Dorran expected to be welcomed by Eli's family with open arms. They'd been nice enough when he and Eli had been friends as teenagers, but Dorran didn't fool himself into thinking they would have continued to allow him into their home if they'd known what kind of relationship he'd had with their son. The same would happen now. They might welcome him if Eli told them they were friends again, but Dorran had no doubt they'd kick him out if Eli told them that they were boyfriends.

So why did he want them to know?

It wasn't an easy question to answer, but he did know that it wasn't his place to make that decision.

He closed the door, signaling that Eli was welcome to stay. "I was watching a movie."

"I can stay?"

It wasn't often that Eli sounded so hesitant. "Of course you can. You're my boyfriend, aren't you?"

Eli caught Dorran's hand and pulled him closer. "I am. And I'm sorry this can't be easier. Trust me, I hate having to be careful about what I say to them. I hate not having you by my side on Sunday lunch while my brothers can bring their wife and girlfriend without even having to think about it."

Dorran stepped into Eli's arms. He closed his eyes and took a deep breath, reminding himself why he was with Eli.

He loved Eli. Eli was a good man. He worked hard to bring justice to the victims of the crimes he investigated. He could be hard and uncompromising, but it wasn't anything Dorran couldn't deal with. He could also be sweet and gentle, and those were the moments Dorran treasured.

He could too easily imagine what his life without Eli would be, and he didn't want to live it. He wasn't sure how long he could push through, but he was going to try. He and Eli had a second chance, and Dorran didn't want to waste it. He didn't want to lose it, not without trying as hard as he could to make things work.

"Why don't we watch the rest of the movie? Or I can put it back to the beginning if you want," he said, stepping away.

"Nah. I'm beat. We can finish watching it and go to bed."

Dorran nodded and went back to sit on the couch, Eli next

to him. He settled against Eli's side, but things between them felt fragile, as if a word or a small movement could break them.

Something — someone — squeezed Dorran's shoulder. He didn't have to check to know Francis was invisible again, and he was grateful. For all that Francis enjoyed teasing Eli, he knew when not to push, when to leave Dorran and Eli alone to solve their problems, or at the very least, not make them worse.

Things were not okay, but Dorran could fake it for one night. He could deal with his feelings tomorrow.

CHAPTER THREE

Dorran didn't want to open the door. He knew who it was—he and Carole had decided to meet today so she could help him train—but he wasn't in the mood, not when things between him and Eli were still awkward.

It had been a few days since they'd made up, and while they were faking it the best they could—or at least Dorran was faking it—it wasn't the same. It didn't *feel* the same.

So the only thing Dorran wanted to do was hide in his apartment and try to focus on his work. He'd forgotten that Carole was going to come by, or he'd have called her to ask her to reschedule. It was too late now, though.

"Dorran? I can hear you in there," she called from the other side of the door.

Dorran was pretty sure Francis had just told her he was hovering there. He wasn't making any noise because he'd been hoping she might leave if he didn't answer.

He huffed and opened the door. "Hi."

Carole arched a blond brow. "Hi? That's all you have to say? Why were you hiding, Dorran?"

"I wasn't hiding." He let Carole in. "I was just coming to open."

"That's not what Francis said."

Dorran scowled. Of course Francis was invisible right now, so Dorran couldn't glare at him. He had no doubt the ghost could see him, though. "Francis doesn't know what he's talking about."

"So everything is fine and dandy?"

Dorran wanted to lie to her, but he didn't. She'd probably find out the truth from Francis anyway. "No. That doesn't mean I was hiding."

Carole put her bag onto Dorran's couch. "What's going on, Dorran?"

"Nothing you can help me with. I'm not sure I'm up to doing this right now, though."

Carole sighed. "If you're not feeling well, we can reschedule, but you can't keep on wasting time, Dorran."

Dorran crossed his arms over his chest. "I'm not wasting time."

"Maybe not on purpose. But you *have* to learn how to use and control your psychic power before it gets out of control."

Dorran wasn't sure he wanted an answer, but he still asked, "What would happen if it did?" He liked being able to communicate with Francis, but he had no intention of using his so-called ability in any other way. It had been freaky enough when his brother's dead girlfriend had appeared in front of him to tell him Chris hadn't killed her. He wasn't looking forward to something like that happening again.

Carole sat on the couch. "I know that right now, it feels like your power is nice, that it's useful. But it's going to become stronger over time."

"Why? If I don't exercise it, it should lessen, right?"

"That's not how it works. Whatever happened to unlock your power, it's a done thing. It's going to get stronger as the time passes, and if you don't learn how to use it and how to control it, the ghosts are going to take over. You're lucky that Francis likes you. He's managed to keep the other ghosts out of your apartment until now, and I'm going to give you a few things to shield this place so they won't be able to sneak in. But you need to learn how to push them away and close your mind off to them, Dorran."

Dorran blinked. "Francis has been keeping other ghosts

17

away?" He wasn't surprised there *were* other ghosts in the building. He knew of at least one person other than Francis who'd died there, and he hoped John Mitchell would never manage to find a way in.

"He has. Are you ready to work on this?"

Dorran sighed. He wasn't ready to do anything but mope around, but he was an adult. He had things to do, and this was one of them. "Yeah, okay." Maybe it would distract him from Eli and the clusterfuck that their relationship had become.

Carole nodded. She toed off her shoes and slid to the floor, pushing the coffee table to the side until there was enough space for both her and Dorran to sit cross-legged facing each other. "Come on. Join me."

Dorran mirrored her position. The floor was hard under his ass, but he kept his mouth shut.

"All right," Carole said. "Now close your eyes and empty your mind."

"Are we meditating?"

"We are."

"Why?"

"Because it will help you learn how to control what you see. Now shut up and do what I told you to do."

Dorran closed his eyes. Carole knew what she was doing. From what Dorran knew, she'd been working as a medium for a while, and she'd been able to help him learn to talk with Francis. If she was right and Dorran needed to learn control to avoid being swamped by ghosts, then Dorran would do whatever she asked of him. He had enough problems as it was with Francis hanging around the apartment.

Dorran wasn't sure how long it was before Carole spoke again. He'd been doing his best to do what she asked, and he'd found meditating surprisingly peaceful.

"How many ghosts are in the room with us, Dorran?"

Carole asked.

"Francis," Dorran answered without thinking about it.

"Are you sure there's only him?"

Dorran wasn't. "How do I find out if there are others?"

"Reach out with your mind. You know what ghosts feel like."

"I actually don't."

"You might not be aware of it, but you do. You wouldn't be able to tell me Francis is here otherwise."

The reason Dorran had mentioned Francis was that Francis hardly ever left the apartment, but he decided to keep that to himself. He wasn't sure what to do — Carole's explanation wasn't as helpful as Dorran wished it was — but he tried.

And sure enough, there *was* someone else. Dorran opened his eyes, blinking at the sunlight. Francis was there, perched on the back of the couch, but he wasn't alone. An older woman was sitting on the couch, looking like she'd rather be anywhere but there. "Oh. Who's that?"

Carole opened her eyes and grimaced. "My aunt. She likes to follow me around when I work."

"She doesn't look happy."

"She never is."

"And who's fault is that, boy?" Carole's aunt snapped.

Dorran was slightly offended at being called *boy* by her until he realized she was staring at Carole.

Carole rolled her eyes. "No one asked you to follow me around. You can stay at home instead of being with me. Wouldn't it be nice for both of us, since you can't stand me?"

"Someone has to warn the people you're fooling them. They have to be aware of what you are."

Dorran felt like he probably shouldn't be listening to this conversation. Was this what his life was going to be from now on? Was he going to have to stand there while people fought with their ghosts?

"I'm not fooling anyone, auntie. You know it. I really do see you."

"That's not what I was talking about." The aunt waved at Carole. "*That's* what I'm talking about. Behaving like a woman. Dressing like one. Bah."

Dorran wasn't sure he wanted to continue listening to the aunt. "How do I stop seeing and hearing her?" he asked Carole, careful not to look at her aunt.

"Oh, you don't want to see me anymore, boy?" the woman asked. "But I'll still be there. I need to be. I have to warn people about Carl."

"I have no idea who you're talking about."

"Close your eyes again," Carole said.

Dorran obeyed. He was eager not to have to listen to that woman again.

"Now push her presence away. It's going to become easier for you to shut the ghosts out as the time passes, but you'll have to train."

"How do I push her away?"

"Try to imagine yourself touching her and doing just that."

Dorran felt weird, but what did he know? He visualized his hands in his mind. And using them, he pushed Carole's aunt away. He hoped it would work, and when he opened his eyes and saw that only Francis was there, he was relieved. Francis waved at him and disappeared, and Dorran allowed himself to relax. "What was that about?" he asked.

Carole got up and smoothed her jeans over her thighs. "She never accepted that I felt I wasn't born the right gender."

"Oh."

Carole smiled. "I'm a transgender woman, Dorran."

"I see." Dorran wasn't sure what else to say. He didn't care about that, and it was weird to think that someone cared so much so that they'd stuck around after dying just to make sure—well, Dorran wasn't even sure what. Did Carole's aunt go around warning people about her? How was she doing that, since she was a ghost? It was true that most ghosts could make themselves visible if they tried and if they'd been dead long enough, but it seemed like a waste of time to do it for this.

"Don't worry about her. I'm used to having her around. She hasn't left my side since she died six years ago."

"You know I don't care, right?"

Carole smiled. "That's good to know. And what's even better to know is that you're actually doing great at controlling your power."

"I didn't do anything."

"You did. And you'll get better as you train. It'll also be easier for you to replicate what you did today."

"It wasn't hard, but I felt kind of stupid."

"That's going to pass, too. You need to accept this as a part of yourself because it is. There's no coming back from it."

That was what Dorran was afraid of.

Dorran was still shaken by what had happened that afternoon when someone knocked on his door. He glared at it from his spot on the couch. He knew it couldn't be Carole — she wouldn't torture him twice in a day, and she'd said he needed to rest and practice talking with Francis — and he hoped it wasn't Emanuel. He didn't feel to chatting with him, not tonight.

He suspected it was Eli, and he was right. Eli stood there when Dorran opened the door, looking just as tired as he had when he'd left the apartment two mornings previous after they'd spent the night together. They'd only slept, or in Dorran's case, he'd tried to sleep, but he couldn't help but feel like they were barreling toward the end of their relationship even though neither of them wanted that.

"Eli. What are you doing here?" Dorran asked before he

could think better of it.

"You sound like you're not happy to see me."

"I am. I'm just tired." And as he let Eli in, he couldn't help but wonder if they were about to start fighting.

It was Sunday. That meant that unless he'd been called into work, Eli had spent lunch and part of the afternoon at his parents' house. Dorran desperately wanted to ask what had happened, but he knew better. The only answers he would get would be annoyance and maybe a grunt or two. Eli didn't like to talk about his parents, not with Dorran, and since they'd reached a tentative peace when it came to Eli's family, Dorran decided not to push. Still, since he wanted Eli to remember what they'd talked about the last time they'd seen each other, he asked, "What did you do today? You could have come over earlier." He sat back on the couch and waited.

Eli shrugged off his jacket. "You know where I was. Why don't you come out and ask what you want to know?"

Of course Eli knew. He didn't have to be a detective to be able to read Dorran. They knew each other too well. "How are your parents?" Dorran could ask about them without fighting with Eli, or at least, he hoped so. He also hoped the resentment he felt wasn't evident in his voice.

Eli flopped onto the couch and took his shoes off, then his socks. "They're okay. Dad's leg hurts, but he won't see a doctor. He says it's the old age."

Dorran couldn't help but smile. "He's not that old."

"Sixty-one."

"Like I said, not that old."

"Mom will convince him to go sooner or later. You know how she is. Besides, his age isn't the problem."

Dorran *had* known her, but he wasn't sure he did anymore. It had been a long time ago, and things had no doubt changed. "Yeah. Why are you here, Eli?"

Eli leaned back against the couch. "I thought we were

okay."

"We are." Mostly.

"Then it's not a problem for me to visit my boyfriend, is it? Or do I need a reason to do it?"

"You don't." Dorran hated this situation. He was torn between wanting to shut up so Eli would stay with him and wanting to ask him what he was planning to do. Eli had asked for more time, though, and Dorran could give him that, at least for a bit.

Eli smiled. "Good. What are you watching?"

"I have no idea. I turned the TV on, but I was thinking about the book I'm translating right now." He knew better than to go into details about that. Eli would listen, but his eyes usually glazed over when Dorran talked about the problems he had with his translations.

Eli grinned. "Want to cuddle?"

"Why don't we go to bed? You have to get up early tomorrow morning, so it would be better not to stay up late."

"I like the way you think."

Dorran got up, but Eli snatched him by the waist and pulled him into his lap. Dorran went. He *wanted* to go. He wanted to feel close to Eli again and to forget they were fighting.

He wrapped his arms around Eli's neck and leaned close. His heart shouldn't be racing the way it was. It wasn't the first time Eli kissed him. It *felt* like a first time of sorts, though, and Dorran allowed himself to sink into the feeling.

Would it be so bad never to meet Eli's family as his boyfriend? He could have this—Eli coming over at night, staying with him, meeting with their friends for a beer. It was only Eli's parents they were hiding from, after all. Eli was out at work, although he wasn't exactly flaunting being gay. But his partner knew, and he hadn't had anything to say about it when Dorran had met him.

Eli manhandled Dorran until he straddled his lap. When he reached into Dorran's pajama pants, Dorran closed his eyes and focused on the feeling of Eli's hand on his cock, of being in Eli's arms.

"God, I've missed you," Eli murmured against Dorran's mouth.

"I missed you, too." Dorran had, and he didn't want to think about how much he'd miss Eli if they broke up, so instead of doing that, he focused on Eli. He unbuttoned Eli's shirt as fast as he could and pushed it off his chest and under his arms. Then he rubbed his hand over Eli's skin, down to his pants.

It was awkward, but neither of them cared. Dorran managed to open Eli's pants and pull his cock out just as Eli pushed Dorran's pajama pants down as much as he could, hooking them under Dorran's balls. The pressure went straight to Dorran's head, igniting the pleasure that had been lurking in his groin ever since Eli had pulled him onto his lap.

Dorran scrambled to wrap his hand around his and Eli's cocks. His fingers weren't long enough, but with Eli's help, they managed to find a rhythm that worked for both of them. It had only been a week or so since the last time they'd had sex, yet it had felt like an eternity. Dorran clutched Eli's shoulder with his free hand, holding on for dear life as Eli brought both of them to orgasm.

Dorran didn't let go, not even once they'd both come and his t-shirt was dirty with their release. He wasn't sure he *could* let go, not when he was terrified that what he had with Eli might be about to end.

Eli stroked Dorran's back and held him. "I'm not going anywhere," he murmured.

Of course he knew what Dorran was feeling. "You can't know that."

"Yeah, I can. I'm telling you, it's going to take more than a few fights for me to let you go. I did that when we were kids, and I'm not going to do it again, not now that I have you back."

Dorran wished he could believe him.

The ringing woke Dorran up. He blinked, his brain not understanding why the bedroom was dark. Why would anyone be at his door in the middle of the night? It wasn't Eli, because he was right there next to Dorran, surprisingly still asleep even through the ruckus. That alone was enough for Dorran to realize how tired he'd been when he'd arrived last night, and he was glad they were sharing his bed.

The ringing didn't stop. Dorran swore, vowing to strangle whoever was making this much noise at . . . one AM? *For fuck's sake.*

Dorran got out of bed. He didn't want Eli to wake up, not if he could avoid it. It was a small miracle that he hadn't jumped out of bed at the first ring.

The bell was still ringing when he got to the door. He thought he heard something behind him, maybe Eli waking up — he wouldn't have been surprised — but he ignored it and swung the door open. His lips were already forming the words *what the fuck*, but they never got out.

Emanuel was standing on Dorran's doorstep. His hair was wild around him, and his eyes were wide — and he was holding a bloody knife.

"Emanuel?" Dorran managed to get out.

Emanuel thrust the knife into Dorran's hands. "I found it under my couch. I didn't do anything, I swear."

Chapter Four

"**D**on't touch it!" Eli snapped.

Dorran dropped the knife, but it was too late. His hands were stained with the blood that had been on it, even though it was mostly dry. And it *was* blood. He could smell it, the coppery scent making him want to throw up. He also wanted to scrub his hands, but he knew better.

Eli appeared next to him. "Damn it, Dorran."

"I'm sorry. I was so surprised that I didn't react in time."

Eli glared at Emanuel, who was shivering just outside the door. His gaze softened when he turned back to Dorran. "Stay here, both of you. And don't touch anything."

Since Dorran wasn't about to get anything dirty with the blood on his hand, he was on board with that.

Eli disappeared into the kitchen. Dorran looked at Emanuel, but he wasn't sure what to say to him. He was shaken, and Dorran wanted to comfort him, but how? He didn't even know what had happened.

Eli reappeared only moments later. He was holding a transparent bag like the ones Dorran used to freeze stuff. He turned it around, wearing it like a glove, and picked up the knife, wrapping it into the bag and closing it.

Once the bag was on the coffee table, Eli snapped several pictures of Dorran's hands and even got a few samples of the blood on them with q-tips.

Then, finally, he told Dorran he could wash his hands. "I called work. They're sending someone to grab the evidence, but my boss doesn't see a problem with me asking questions.

They'll probably want to get your prints, just because you touched the knife, but since I can testify as to where you were the entire night and how your hands got on that knife, you shouldn't be in trouble."

Dorran rushed into the kitchen, turned on the water in the sink with his elbows, and started scrubbing. "What about Emanuel?" The area in front of the sink was open, so Dorran could see him hovering at the door. He'd stepped in, but he looked like he had no idea what to do.

Eli swore. "Okay, let's do this again."

He was surprisingly gentle as he guided Emanuel toward the couch and made him sit, careful not to have his hands touch anything. Then he did what he'd done with Dorran, snapping pictures of Emanuel's hands with his phone and taking samples. "Can you tell me what happened?" he asked as Dorran was drying his hands and making sure all the blood was gone.

"I don't know."

"How did you get that knife?"

Emanuel blinked. He reached up to push his hair away from his face, but Eli stopped him, grabbing his wrists. Dorran wasn't even surprised he was wearing gloves. He probably always had a pair on him or something.

"Emanuel?" Eli said. "How did you get that knife? Is someone hurt?"

Emanuel shook his head. "I don't know. I found it under my couch."

Eli looked at Dorran, a question in his gaze. Dorran had no idea what he wanted him to say, but he nodded. That was the same thing Emanuel had told him earlier.

Eli nodded. "All right. I called work. A few technicians are coming. They'll make sure I got everything I should have from your hands, and they'll check your apartment. Do you have someone we can call? Your parents, or maybe a boyfriend?"

Emanuel closed his eyes. "My boyfriend."

"Do you have his number?"

"It's in my phone."

"And your phone is . . ."

"In my pocket."

Emanuel had to wiggle a bit so that a now gloveless Eli could get his hand into his pocket to take his phone. Eli tried to call Emanuel's boyfriend, but he didn't answer, so he put the phone down. "You said you left your apartment tonight?" he asked.

Dorran wished he could do more. He wanted to help Emanuel, but he couldn't, not until the crime scene technicians arrived and gave him the okay to shower. He couldn't even go grab clean clothes for Emanuel, because until the apartment was cleared, it was a crime scene.

"I went out. I was supposed to meet my boyfriend, but he texted me to cancel. I painted for a while, but I was out of soda, so I went to get a drink."

"When did you come back?"

"I don't know what time it is, but it was right before I found the knife."

"Can you tell me what happened?"

"I walked into my apartment. I had my keys in my hand, and I dropped them next to the couch. I knew that if I didn't pick them up, I'd end up losing them, so I reached down, but I had kicked them under the couch. I had to lay on the floor to look under it. That's when I noticed there was something else there. I thought it was one of the things I lost. I do that often. So I took it out. That's when I saw the blood." He stopped and swallowed. "I didn't know what to do."

"Why did you decide to come to Dorran?"

"It wasn't him I came to. I know the two of you had a fight, but I was hoping you'd be here and that you'd know what to do."

Eli patted Emanuel's knee. "You did the right thing."

Except when he'd handed Dorran the knife and Dorran had stupidly taken it. Dorran hoped that wouldn't be a problem. He could do without being suspected of a crime, even though so far, they had no idea what crime the knife had been involved in. The fact that Emanuel himself had no idea what was going on was worrying. How had that knife ended up under his couch? Who'd put it there?

A knock on the door—Dorran was starting to hate that sound—startled him out of his thoughts. Eli was still busy with Emanuel, so Dorran went to open. He was only mildly surprised to see Mel there. Mel was Eli's partner, so it made sense that Eli had called him. "Where are the others?" he asked as he stepped to the side.

"I don't know. Probably not far behind me. What happened?"

Dorran rubbed his face. His eyes burned and he wanted to go back to bed, but instead, he guided Mel to the kitchen so he could make coffee. "I have no idea. Eli and I were sleeping, someone started ringing at the door, and when I opened, Emanuel thrust a bloody knife in my hands."

Mel grimaced. "Not the best way to wake up."

"Definitely not. And I'm sorry Eli called you."

"My wife and I are used to late-night calls, don't worry. You have no idea who the blood could belong to?"

"No. Emanuel lives on his own. He has a boyfriend, but I didn't hear anything weird tonight, and the blood on the knife was still wet enough in some spots that it stained my hands. There's no way it had been there long."

"Do you know where your friend's boyfriend is?"

"Again, no idea. I don't think I've ever even seen the guy. From what I know, he and Emanuel haven't been together long, so they're not involved much."

"All right. Why don't we sit down so I can write down what you just told me."

Dorran groaned. Mel gave him an understanding smile, but it didn't help. "Why do these things follow me around?" Dorran complained.

"You do seem to be a magnet for trouble. You're lucky you're dating a cop, I guess."

Mel was probably right. Dorran imagined he'd have been arrested a few times already if it wasn't for Eli and the fact that he'd turned a blind eye more than once when Dorran was sticking his nose where he shouldn't have.

Dorran was done with that, though. He didn't care whose blood was on the knife. He was *not* going to try to find out what happened. That was Eli and Mel's job, not his, and for once, he was sticking to that decision.

Dorran led Emanuel to the bathroom. He was finally allowed to wash the blood from his hands now that the crime scene technicians had taken all the samples they needed. One of them had looked like she wanted to strangle Eli after she found out he'd allowed Dorran to wash up, but Eli had handed her the bags with the knife and the q-tips he'd used on Dorran, and she'd softened. Not by much, and not enough to stop glaring at him, but Dorran was too tired to care right then. Besides, he wasn't the one who would have to work with her again, and he was glad Eli had allowed him to wash his hands.

"I never use the guest bathroom, so take as much time as you need to shower, okay?" he told Emanuel. This bathroom was almost exactly like the one attached to the master bedroom, and Dorran made sure to keep it stocked in soap and towels, just in case, but he had yet to have anyone sleep there, except maybe Francis. Who knew where and what he did when he wasn't communicating with Dorran. He definitely didn't use the soap, though.

Emanuel nodded. "Thank you."

"I'll go grab some sweats and a t-shirt from my closet. I'll leave them on the bed, so feel free to go to sleep once you're done. I'll see you in the morning."

Emanuel cracked a smile. "It's already morning."

"I guess it is. I won't bother you, so sleep as much as you want."

Emanuel nodded. "Thank you, Dorran."

"You don't have to thank me. We're friends." Although Dorran wished he could do more for Emanuel. He hadn't even been able to contact his boyfriend, although that was probably because it was the middle of the night — going on early morning by now — and the man was no doubt sleeping. Dorran wished he were.

He left Emanuel to his shower and went back to the living room, where Eli and Mel were talking. They were both sipping coffee, and Dorran wondered if Eli would be able to go back to sleep. Knowing him, he'd want to go to work as soon as possible, even though he hadn't slept more than a few hours.

Dorran knew something was wrong as soon as Eli looked at him. His stomach churned, and while he didn't want to ask this, he had to. "What happened?"

"What did Emanuel tell you about his boyfriend?"

"Not a lot. What happened, Eli? You can ask me all the questions you want after you tell me."

"Emanuel's boyfriend is dead."

Dorran had expected it when Eli hadn't answered him right away. That didn't mean he didn't feel the need to sit down to try to wrap his mind around the news. "What happened? Can you tell me more?"

Eli and Mel exchanged a glance. Mel shrugged, and while Dorran wasn't sure what that meant, Eli seemed to understand. He turned to look at Dorran. "I asked Emanuel about his boyfriend tonight, mostly because I thought he probably needed someone to comfort him. I didn't think much of the fact that the boyfriend didn't answer the phone until Mel told me there'd been a murder earlier tonight. The man was stabbed."

"You checked because of the knife." It made sense, and it was what Dorran would have done.

"Yes. We checked the names, and they're the same."

"Axel Ford."

Eli nodded again. He moved jerkily, and Dorran wasn't sure if it was because this case was hitting close to home or because he was tired. He needed more sleep, but Dorran knew better than to bring that up right now.

Dorran sighed. "Are you going to tell Emanuel? I don't think he's in bed yet."

"Not right now."

That made Dorran frown until he realized what was going on. "You can't think he did it."

Eli's expression was enough to tell Dorran that yes, that was what he thought, or at the very least, it was an option he couldn't ignore. "You have to see how it looks, Dorran."

Dorran couldn't deny that. Emanuel and his boyfriend were supposed to see each other. They hadn't—from what Emanuel had said—and Emanuel had spent the evening and the night on his own. Someone might have seen him at the store, but that didn't mean he hadn't had the time to kill his boyfriend, go have a drink to make sure people noticed him, then go home and *find* the knife.

It was possible, but Dorran couldn't imagine Emanuel doing something like that. Even though he hadn't been in love with his boyfriend—and wasn't that a point in his favor? Why kill his boyfriend if he didn't have strong feelings for him— he'd still liked the guy, and he just wasn't the kind of person who could be cold enough to plan and do something like this.

Mel cleared his throat. "No one is saying your friend did anything wrong."

Dorran snorted. "Eli is."

"No, he's not. No one here can deny how bad things are looking for your friend, but that doesn't mean he had anything to do with his boyfriend's death. We won't solve anything by fighting right now. We all need more sleep. Things will look better in the morning."

Dorran doubted that, and he wasn't sure he'd manage to sleep after everything, but no matter what Eli thought right now, Dorran wanted to take care of him. This wasn't the right moment to fight with him, especially not over this.

"I'll talk to Emanuel in the morning," Eli said.

Dorran knew it was a big favor. He could have gone to Emanuel right now and taken him to the station. Hell, he probably *should* do that, and Dorran suspected that the main reason he didn't was him. He didn't want to hurt Dorran or have a fight.

That sapped the fight from Dorran. He was tired, and his heart still hurt over the arguments he'd had with Eli. He didn't want to say something he'd regret, and the best way to avoid that was to go to bed.

Mel got up. "I'll see you in the morning."

"Do you want to be here when I talk to Emanuel?" Eli asked.

Mel shook his head. "Don't worry about that. I'll head to the crime scene first thing and see what I can find out. I'm not sure it's a good idea to ask for it to be assigned to us, though. You know Emanuel."

"I do, but he's not a friend. If anything, he doesn't like me at all because he was a suspect in John Mitchell's death. I'll talk to the captain tomorrow, if it makes you feel better."

"It does. See what he says. Now go to bed, both of you. You

look like you're about to fall asleep on your feet."

Dorran saw Mel out. He wasn't surprised to find Eli still on the couch once he'd locked the door, but he *was* surprised when Eli told him he'd sleep there. "I'm sorry, but I need to keep an eye on Emanuel and make sure he doesn't try to sneak out."

"He won't. He doesn't even know about his boyfriend yet."

"Maybe not. I still have to do this."

Dorran sighed. He was annoyed, but he understood. Eli seemed surprised when Dorran brought him a pillow and a blanket, but Dorran was too tired to wonder why. He handed them off and went to bed.

He wasn't sure he'd be able to sleep, not with a thousand questions swirling in his mind and things still uneasy between himself and Eli. His eyes drifted closed as soon as his head hit the pillow, though, and he was more than happy to let sleep take over.

CHAPTER FIVE

Dorran was *not* happy. He was grumpy and sleepy, and those were two things he never dealt with well.

He'd slept last night after Mel had left, but only fitfully. He hadn't been able to stop dreaming about Emanuel holding the knife and *blood*, and that wasn't the best way to rest, which was probably why he felt like he hadn't slept in a week. His eyes burned, and he kept on yawning.

He needed coffee.

Luckily for him, Eli had gotten up before him, and there was a pot ready when he shuffled into the kitchen. He ignored Eli—who was sitting at the table sipping from his own cup— and grabbed an empty mug from the cupboard.

"How did you sleep?" Eli asked after Dorran had taken the first sip.

"It's a miracle I *did* sleep."

Eli grimaced. "I'm sorry."

What could Dorran say to that? It wasn't like what had happened with Emanuel was Eli's fault. "It's fine. Is he still in the bedroom?"

"I haven't heard anything from there yet. I didn't expect you to get up this early."

Dorran peered at the watch on his wrist. It was going on ten AM, which after the night he'd had was way too early for him to be awake, let alone to have a conscious thought. "I didn't want to get up, but I couldn't sleep anymore."

Eli nodded. He'd showered—and how hadn't Dorran heard him coming and going to the bathroom in his bedroom—and he was wearing a clean shirt. He didn't have a tie on yet, but Dorran knew he would when he left the apartment.

That thought reminded Dorran of Emanuel. "Should I go wake him up? Have you heard anything from Mel yet?"

"He talked to our captain. He's still not sure it's a good idea for me to take this investigation, but I want to, and Emanuel and I aren't close. We barely know each other. That means I won't be biased."

"Are you sure about that? He's a friend of mine."

Eli peered at Dorran over the rim of his mug. "Are the two of you close? You never told me about it. But he did say he knew we'd been fighting."

Dorran forced himself not to look down. "Not because I told him. He heard us the other day, and when we met in the hallway, he asked me about it."

"Did you tell him?"

"Yeah, a bit."

"So you're close."

"Not really. We don't usually talk. He just happened to be there and ask. That's how I knew he had a boyfriend. I don't know anything else about him, though, not beyond a normal chat with a neighbor."

Eli nodded. "I'll bring it up to the captain, but it shouldn't be a problem. You're not best friends, and even though he came here last night, he admitted it was because he thought he'd find me, not because he was looking for you."

Dorran was mostly relieved that Eli would take care of this. Eli could be stubborn when he wanted to, but he was a good detective, and he'd find the truth. Dorran didn't think Emanuel had anything to do with his boyfriend's death, and Eli would make sure everyone knew that. He had to.

"Good morning," Emanuel said as he walked into the living room. He was wearing Dorran's clothes, but they were short on him. The sweatpants stopped just above his ankles, exposing a stripe of hairy, pale skin. He looked tired, and Dorran doubted he'd slept much more than he had, or better.

He hated that things were about to get worse for him. He looked at Eli, silently asking him when he wanted to tell Emanuel that his boyfriend was dead and that he was the main and, so far, only suspect in the case. If it were him, he'd wait until Emanuel had breakfast, but he doubted Eli would. Knowing him, he'd want to get this out of the way so he could start interrogating Emanuel and investigating the murder as soon as possible. That was a good thing, but Dorran hated that one of his friends was involved. He and Emanuel weren't close, but they knew each other, and Emanuel had given Dorran advice when he'd needed it.

He got another cup of coffee ready while Eli asked Emanuel to sit down. Dorran suspected Emanuel knew something had happened just because of Eli's expression. He looked like he wanted to bolt, and Dorran hoped he wouldn't.

Dorran placed the new cup in front of Emanuel, then hesitated. "Do you need me to leave?" he asked Eli. He wanted to stay to support Emanuel, but if Eli didn't think it was a good idea, he wouldn't. It was Eli's job, and contrary to Dorran, he knew what he was doing.

"You can stay." Eli didn't need to say that Emanuel would probably need the support. Dorran understood.

He sat next to Emanuel, ignoring the man's confused glances. He was glad Eli was the one who would tell Emanuel about his boyfriend. He'd never had to give this kind of news to anyone. Even when his brother's girlfriend had been killed, he'd been called later, after Chris had found out. He wouldn't know where to start.

"I have bad news, unfortunately," Eli said.

Emanuel clutched his cup of coffee. "Did you find out who was hurt with the knife I found?"

37

"We can't be sure it was the knife used, not until the blood is analyzed. But someone did die. I'm sorry, Emanuel. Axel Ford was found dead in his apartment last night."

Dorran wasn't sure what to do. He wanted to comfort Emanuel, but he had no idea how or if Emanuel would actually want that from him.

"He was stabbed?" Emanuel asked.

"Yes."

"With the knife I found."

"Like I said, we can't be sure—"

Emanuel snorted. "Come on. It would be too big a coincidence, wouldn't it? Am I a suspect? Of course I am. Axel gets stabbed, and I find a bloody knife in my apartment. You have to see it was put there, though, right? I wouldn't have been so stupid as to come to a cop with the knife if I'd killed Axel."

Eli raised his hands. "I don't know anything for sure right now. But like you said, things *are* looking bad for you, especially if the blood on the knife belongs to Axel."

Dorran was ready to bet it did. Someone had tried to make it look like Emanuel had killed his boyfriend, and they'd succeeded. Emanuel had spent most of the night alone. No doubt the killer had stabbed Axel during the time Emanuel had been painting in his apartment. Then they'd probably put the knife in his apartment while he was out, and he'd found it at his return.

Everything was neat and would make sure Emanuel was arrested for killing his boyfriend.

"Can you tell me what you did last night again?" Eli asked. At least he sounded gentle and not like he suspected Emanuel.

Emanuel pushed his coffee away. "I spent most of the evening at home. I was supposed to see Axel, but he canceled."

"How?"

"He texted me. You can check my phone."

"I will. So you stayed home?"

"Yeah. I was trying to figure out one of my paintings. I wasn't happy with the way it was coming. So I put in earbuds and got to work. I'm not sure what time it was when I finally stopped, but by the time I washed and got ready to leave, it was just after midnight."

"You went out that late?"

"Yeah. The bar at the corner closes at one. I just wanted a soda, nothing alcoholic, and I didn't have anything at home."

"What time did you get there?"

"I don't know. Ten past midnight, maybe? I got a soda and played with my phone a bit. Then I talked to the bartender. I left just before one and came home. That's when I dropped my keys and found the knife."

Eli had been taking notes, but Dorran doubted he'd forget any of the details. He knew *he* wouldn't, even though he wished he could. He didn't want to be involved in this, not after what he'd gone through. He'd been shot and assaulted, and that had been more than enough to cure him of wanting to help with the investigation.

But Emanuel was a friend, even though they weren't close, and things weren't looking good for him. Dorran didn't want to get involved, but if things went south, he would.

He wouldn't have a choice.

The words weren't making any sense, no matter how hard Dorran focused on them. It was stupid of him even to try, but he'd needed to after Emanuel and Eli had left the apartment. He knew that otherwise, he'd obsess over what was happening, and he didn't want to. But he also couldn't focus on the translation he was supposed to be doing. He was too worried about Emanuel.

Eli had walked him to his apartment after they'd talked

over coffee this morning. He'd allowed Emanuel to dress in his own clothes, but that was it, and he'd taken him to the station after that. Dorran hadn't gone with them—he didn't have a reason to, and he knew Eli wouldn't want him there. If Eli had to be in charge of the investigation, Dorran needed to keep his distance because of the risk that Eli's boss would think he was too close to Emanuel and take him off the case.

It was going to be hell.

Dorran trusted Eli, and he knew his boyfriend was great at his job, but he couldn't help but wonder if maybe the anger Eli and Dorran had toward each other would spill over into the case. It wouldn't be on purpose—Eli would never botch an investigation just because he was fighting with Dorran— but separating things wasn't always that easy, and Dorran was right in the middle of this whether he wanted to be or not. There was no denying that Emanuel had come to him when he'd found the knife, even though he'd been looking for Eli.

Dorran leaned back in his chair and rubbed his face.

He knew how bad things could go even for innocent people. His own brother had almost ended up behind bars for the murder of his girlfriend, and he hadn't done anything. Eli hadn't been in charge of that investigation, but Dorran knew him. He'd follow the rules—as he should—even if it meant locking Emanuel up.

But Dorran didn't believe Emanuel had anything to do with his boyfriend's death. No matter what the evidence said, he couldn't believe it. Emanuel didn't have it in him. He was spoiled and distant when it came to his boyfriend, but that didn't make him a killer. Dorran didn't have all the information, but from what Emanuel had told him, he hadn't been in love with Axel, and while that didn't mean he didn't have a reason to kill him, Dorran doubted he did. When they'd talked, he'd thought Emanuel sounded neutral about Axel, as if being with him didn't matter much. As if he was with him more because he didn't want to be alone than because he loved him.

So why would he kill him? And why would he bring the knife to Dorran knowing Eli might be there? Why would he keep the knife in the first place? That didn't make sense, no matter how much Dorran thought about it. What could he do to help Emanuel, though?

Dorran wouldn't be allowed to talk to him if he was arrested, but hopefully, Emanuel would come home at the end of the day, and they could talk. Dorran didn't think Emanuel could tell him more than he already knew, though. Who else could?

Dorran knew. He'd been trying not to think about it because he didn't want to do it, but it would be the easiest way to find out what had happened. He wouldn't be able to prove anything, but at least he'd know.

But Dorran wanted nothing less than to contact Axel's ghost and ask him who had killed him.

Most days, he barely tolerated Francis, and they'd been sharing the apartment ever since Dorran had moved in. Dorran hadn't minded seeing the ghost of his brother's girlfriend, because she'd helped him be sure Chris didn't have anything to do with her death, and in a way, she'd been family.

Axel wasn't. Dorran had never met him when he'd been alive, and he didn't think he would have even if he hadn't been killed. From what Emanuel had said, Dorran doubted he and Axel would have stayed together for long.

But Dorran *needed* to do it. He had to know what happened, because it would be his only way to help Emanuel. He wasn't even sure why it was so important to him except that he liked Emanuel, and he could see them becoming friends if they had the opportunity to spend time together. But even if that never happened, Emanuel didn't deserve to spend any length of time behind bars, because he hadn't killed his boyfriend. Dorran was sure of that, and helping Emanuel get out of this was the right thing to do. Dorran wouldn't be able to forgive himself if he didn't do whatever he could to help.

He sighed and grabbed his phone. He knew what he had to do, but he didn't think he could do it on his own, not yet. He dialed Carole's number. Eli was going to be pissed, but Dorran was ready to stand his ground.

"Dorran, hi," Carole said when she answered.

"Carole, I need your help."

"You need to relax and focus, Dorran."

Dorran knew Carole was right, but that didn't make it easier. He hadn't been able to focus on his work that afternoon, and he couldn't focus on emptying his mind tonight. The fact that he expected Eli to come by and find Carole there with him didn't help. Dorran knew Eli wouldn't be happy, especially when he found out why Carole was there. He hoped they wouldn't fight again, but he wouldn't be surprised if they did. It seemed that was their preferred way to go about things lately, and while it was partially his fault, it was Eli's too.

"Dorran!" Carole snapped.

Right. He was supposed to focus. "Sorry."

"I understand you're shaken, but if you want to do this, you're going to have to try to push your worries to the side, at least for the next half hour. Otherwise, you won't be able to contact the man you're looking for. Which is okay, but I know it's important to you, so you need to try."

She was right, so Dorran screwed his eyes shut and tried to stop thinking. He visualized darkness and only that.

"All right. What do you know about this man?" Carole asked, her voice so soft that it was easy to stay focused.

"His name."

Carole tsked. "It's not going to be easy to get him here only with that."

"Is there another way to do this?"

"We could ask Francis to help. He did with your brother's girlfriend, right?"

"Yes."

"Try that, then. Ask Francis to come around."

That was easy enough. Dorran had been training to do that ever since he and Carole had started working together, and since Francis was usually around the apartment, it didn't take a lot of energy and focus to get him to the living room.

Sure enough, when Dorran opened his eyes, Francis was leaning against the side of the couch, his arms crossed over his chest. He grinned at Dorran, and Dorran couldn't help but smile back. "Hey, Francis."

Francis opened his mouth to answer, and to Dorran's shock, actual *words* came out. "Hello, Dorran."

Dorran stared. He'd never heard Francis, either because Francis was still a recent ghost or because the emerging of Dorran's power was so new. The why didn't matter—Dorran could hear Francis now.

"What's wrong with him?" Francis asked Carole.

Carole smiled. "I don't know, but I think I can guess. Dorran?"

Dorran had to shake himself. "Sorry. I just didn't expect to hear Francis." And he looked so real. He was often visible these days, and sometimes when he was, he looked like he was real. Dorran knew from experience that if he tried to touch him, he wouldn't be able to, but it was hard to believe.

Francis' eyebrows shot up. "You heard me?"

"Yes."

Francis' smile widened. "Well, I'll be damned. It's nice to finally be able to talk to you, Dorran."

Dorran swallowed. He'd already been emotional before,

but this was making things worse. "Yeah, it's good to be able to talk to you."

"Boys? Dorran, I know you and Francis want to talk, but that's not what you were trying to do, and you'll have time later."

Francis grimaced. "Of course. But I'm afraid I can't help you. I already knew you'd try to do this, Dorran, so I attempted to contact Emanuel's boyfriend. I want to help him as much as you do. He's always been a good man."

"He didn't answer?"

"He did, but he just died, and he hasn't quite wrapped his mind around that yet."

Dorran felt sorry for Axel, but that wasn't going to stop him. Emanuel was very much alive, and he needed help more than Axel needed to be handled with kid gloves. "Do you think he'll come if I try to contact him?"

"I have no idea. I'll help if that's what you want, but I doubt you'll get much from him."

"Please. I have to try."

"Close your eyes again," Carole ordered. "Think about Axel."

It was hard, because Dorran didn't even know what the man looked like. He thought about Emanuel, though, and about Axel's name.

"Dorran?" Francis asked.

When Dorran opened his eyes, a man was standing next to Francis. He was handsome, and it was easy to imagine him with Emanuel, even though he looked scared. His eyes were wide as he looked around, and when he tried to touch the couch and couldn't, he freaked out.

Dorran didn't need to be able to hear him to know he was freaking out. It was clear, and it hurt to see it. Dorran wanted to reassure him, but he didn't know how. "Axel?"

Axel turned around suddenly and faced Dorran. Dorran

swallowed, wondering what was about to happen.

"Hi. I'm Dorran. I'm a friend of your boyfriend."

Axel opened his mouth, and Dorran thought he said *Emanuel*, but he couldn't hear anything. He looked at Carole, who was focused on Axel. Dorran couldn't read Axel's lips, but Carole could hear him, and he hoped she'd be able to help.

"He keeps repeating he wants to see Emanuel," she said. "Nothing else."

"Try asking him who killed him."

She did, but from what Dorran could see, Axel never stopped asking for Emanuel. "I'm sorry, Dorran," Carole said, shaking her head.

"But he wants to see Emanuel. That has to mean Emanuel doesn't have anything to do with his death, right?"

"Or that he wants to confront him. There's no way to know for sure, not right now. He's too new, too scared to help us. We'll try again, of course, but right now, I doubt we can get anything else out of him."

Dorran sighed. He'd known it would be a long shot, but he'd hoped to get something else out of this. Carole was right, though. He wasn't giving up, and maybe once Axel was more used to being dead, he'd help them. Thinking that made Dorran feel guilty, but he couldn't do anything to change the fact that Axel was dead.

The sound of a key in the front door lock made all of them jump. Axel disappeared, Francis right behind him as he waved at Dorran. Carole couldn't just fade away, though, so when Eli walked in, she was one of the first things he saw. He wasn't quick enough, and Dorran saw him grimace.

Dorran got up. "Hey. I didn't expect you to come home this early today."

"I noticed."

Dorran's hackles rose, but he tried to stay calm. "Carole and I were talking."

"And since we're done, I'm going to go," Carole said.

Dorran could tell she wanted to get out of Eli's way and give him and Dorran an opportunity to talk. The fact that she knew that Eli didn't like her, or rather, didn't like what she represented, probably had a role in how fast she was leaving, though.

Dorran waited until she was gone to ask, "What happened today, with Emanuel?" He was going to ignore the way Eli was scowling at the front door even though Carole was long gone. He needed to—he needed answers.

"It's none of your business, Dorran."

Dorran jerked back. Eli hadn't hit him, but he might as well have. "I know you're angry because Carole was here, but she's helping me."

"She's feeding you her bullshit about ghosts, you mean."

"Eli, you saw Francis yourself. You can't tell me you don't believe in ghosts."

"Maybe I was wrong. It could have been something else."

Dorran swallowed. "It wasn't, and you know it. Are you saying I'm crazy because I can talk with ghosts?"

"No, but—"

"Then you believe me." Dorran knew Eli didn't *want* to believe him, but there were no two ways about it.

Eli raked a hand through his hair. "I don't want you to see her again."

"And I don't want you to tell me what to do. Tough luck, Eli. I'm an adult. I can make my own decisions."

"Don't you see I'm doing this for you? Because I care?"

"If you cared so much, you wouldn't be hiding me from your family," Dorran snapped before he could think better of it. He groaned. "I'm sorry. I didn't mean to bring this up."

"Yet you did."

"What do you want from me, Eli? I didn't mean to bring it up, but I think about it. How can I not?"

"You know what? I'm going to leave. I don't want to fight with you tonight, Dorran."

Dorran should probably have stopped him, but he didn't. He didn't want to fight, either, and he knew that was where they were heading. He hated it, but he couldn't change it. He was trying to do the right thing. Eli, on the other hand, was trying to keep his world under control, and it wasn't working anymore.

CHAPTER SIX

Emanuel was in jail.

Dorran hadn't noticed at first—he'd been trying to focus on his work, something he hadn't been able to do since the incident with Emanuel that night, so he hadn't left his apartment in a few days. Then he had, and he'd gone to knock on Emanuel's door. He'd felt guilty that he'd basically ignored Emanuel even though the man was a somewhat friend and he'd just lost his boyfriend.

No one had answered, at least not Emanuel's door. The next neighbor over had opened hers, though, and she'd told Dorran Emanuel had been taken to the station earlier that morning. Dorran wasn't sure if it meant he'd been arrested for the murder of his boyfriend, but chances were that he had.

And Dorran didn't know what to do.

He still didn't think Emanuel had anything to do with Axel's death. No matter what Carole had said about Axel wanting to see Emanuel because he'd killed him, Dorran didn't believe it. No one would actively want to see their killer. Of course, Dorran didn't know that much about dead people, but he was a human being just like Axel had been.

Telling the cops Axel's ghost still wanted to see Emanuel wasn't going to cut it, though.

Dorran groaned and looked down at his phone. He and Eli hadn't talked since Eli had stormed out of his apartment after finding him with Carole. Dorran had wanted to call him, but he hadn't been sure what to say. *Sorry I was with Carole?* It wasn't like he'd been cheating on Eli with her, for fuck's sake, and while he understood Eli was uncomfortable with him seeing ghosts, there was nothing he could do about that. Carole had been clear about what would happen if he tried to ignore it, and Dorran wasn't ready to face that.

Dorran bit his lower lip. Between the ghost thing and the thing with Eli's family, it felt more and more like their relationship was slipping away. He didn't like it—he *hated* it—but was there anything he could do? He supposed he could try to avoid talking about Eli's family, but that wouldn't solve the problem. He could hide his chats with ghosts, too, but again, it wouldn't change the fact that he could communicate with them. And now that he could finally hear Francis, Dorran wasn't about to give that up. Francis had been his friend ever since he'd moved in, even though he'd been invisible most of that time.

But Dorran loved Eli. He wanted Eli in his life. Surely there was something they could do to make it work. One of them had to take the first step, though, and since Eli was no doubt swamped with work, it looked like Dorran was going to be the one to do it.

He quickly dialed Eli's number from memory before he could think better of it.

"Detective Hayes."

Dorran blinked. He wasn't sure how to answer—hadn't Eli looked at his screen before answering? Or was he still angry? "Eli?"

"Dorran. I guess you heard about your friend."

Dorran winced. Okay, so maybe he should have thought better about calling now. Of course Eli was going to think he wanted answers, and he did. It just wasn't the only reason he'd called. "I did. I wanted to talk to you, though." He sighed. "I don't like it when we fight."

There was a pause before Eli answered. Maybe he was surprised that Dorran was telling him that instead of behaving as if nothing had happened? They'd tried that a few times, but it hadn't solved their problems, and they wouldn't be able to go forward if they didn't.

"I don't like it either, yet here we are."

"I think we need to talk."

Eli chuckled. "Probably, but will we manage to do it without fighting?"

"I don't know. We can try."

"I want that." Eli cleared his throat. "How about I come by in a few hours? Will I find you home?"

"You know you will. I'm still trying to wrangle this translation into submission."

"That sounded kinkier than you were probably trying to sound."

Dorran laughed. *This* was why he loved Eli. Even though they hadn't yet cleared the air between them, he wasn't the kind of guy who gave Dorran the silent treatment. They might not be sure where they were in the relationship, but Eli would never ignore Dorran the way some of his exes had. Even though they fought, they were adults, and they were trying to work things out.

"I'll see you tonight, Dorran," Eli said, his voice quieter than before.

"I'll be waiting for you." And this time, he'd be alone.

Of course, he hadn't counted on having Francis suddenly appear in the middle of his office dragging Axel around.

Dorran wasn't sure what made him turn around, since he couldn't see the two ghosts' reflections in his computer screen. He just knew he wasn't alone anymore, and that sensation was creepy. He almost jumped when he saw the ghosts. "Jesus, Francis. Are you trying to give me a heart attack?"

Francis cocked a brow. "Well, I wouldn't mind spending some time with you and having someone to share eternity with."

Dorran's cheeks heated. He'd suspected Francis was attracted to him for a while — the fact that Francis used to peek at him and Eli when they made love and to pinch his ass whenever he could were significant clues of that — but Francis had never been so blunt about it. Of course, that was probably because Dorran hadn't been able to hear him until now. "What's going on?" Dorran asked, ignoring Francis' words.

Francis held his thumb up toward Axel. "I don't think Emanuel killed him."

"Okay. I don't think so either. Can he talk now?"

Francis glanced at Axel. The man still looked shell-shocked, and Dorran didn't blame him. He'd be in shock too if he'd been stabbed to death only a few days ago. "Not really. He keeps saying he wants to see Emanuel, as well as another two names. I don't recognize them."

"What names?" Dorran grabbed a piece of paper. He knew nothing about Axel, and he probably should change that if he wanted to help Emanuel.

"Sophie and Scott."

"Do you have any idea who they are?"

"No idea. I don't think he's gotten used to the fact that he's dead yet, so I suspect they're people who were important to him when he was alive."

Dorran could easily believe that. "Thanks, Francis."

Francis' smile was kind. "Don't worry about it. And I'll make myself scarce so you can talk with Eli."

"This is your home, too."

"I know. It doesn't mean my roommate shouldn't have some privacy, especially when it comes to that hunk of your boyfriend."

Dorran threw his pen at Francis' head, but Francis was already gone. It would have passed straight through him anyway, but damn if it didn't feel satisfying. It wasn't enough to distract him for long, though, and by the time Eli arrived,

51

Dorran was a mess. He wanted to help Emanuel, and he wanted to fix things with Eli. He wasn't sure which one he'd manage tonight — if he managed even one of them. When had his life become so complicated?

Eli settled onto the couch. Dorran wasn't sure where to sit — next to him? They hadn't made peace yet, but he'd missed Eli, and he wanted to be close to him.

"Your friend was arrested this morning," Eli said before Dorran could decide what he wanted to start with.

Dorran almost smiled. "You mean, you and Mel arrested him."

"We did. I'm sorry."

Dorran sighed. "You're doing your job. I take it he's the main suspect?" It was easier to talk about Emanuel than it was to talk about them and their relationship.

"He is." Eli leaned back against the couch. "Between the fact that Axel was his boyfriend, the fact that their relationship wasn't a great one, and the knife, it was a no-brainer. It doesn't mean he did it, of course, but I couldn't *not* arrest him." He looked like he expected Dorran to be angry, and while Dorran *was*, it wasn't at him. Eli was doing his job. He needed time to investigate, but most people probably wanted this solved as soon as possible.

"Is there anything I can do to help him without bugging you and Mel?"

Eli snorted. "When has that stopped you? But maybe. I can give you his lawyer's number. I doubt he's going to stay in for long, not with that shark on his side."

That was good to know. Maybe Emanuel had called his father to ask for help. Dorran didn't know what kind of relationship they had, but he suspected it wasn't great. From what Emanuel has said, his father didn't care much for him. Hopefully that had changed, because Emanuel needed all the help he could get right now.

CHAPTER SEVEN

Things between Dorran and Eli were still fragile—Eli had apparently accepted that Dorran was going to stick his nose into his case no matter what he said or did, but they hadn't yet talked about his family, and really, what was there to say? Dorran had already told Eli how he felt about being kept a secret, and Eli had already told him he needed more time. They just had to manage not to fight in the meantime, which Dorran thought they could do, since Eli was spending a lot of time working and not a lot of it with him. Dorran didn't berate him for that—he'd known what he was getting into when he'd agreed to date Eli—but he missed his boyfriend.

Still, he hoped his path wouldn't cross with Eli's today, because even though Eli didn't seem to have a problem with Dorran helping Emanuel, Dorran knew better than to think he was okay with it.

"Dorran?"

Dorran looked up. Seeing Emanuel dressed in the prison uniform was a shock, and he wanted to bundle the man up and sneak him out. Wasn't his lawyer working on that? Couldn't he get Emanuel out on a bond or something? Dorran obviously should pay more attention when he watched those real-crime TV series.

"What are you doing here?" Emanuel asked, sliding into the seat in front of Dorran.

"I wanted to make sure you were okay."

Emanuel snorted. "Do I look like I'm okay? I'm in fucking

53

jail, Dorran." His accent was coming out more strongly now.

"I'm sorry."

Emanuel rubbed his face. "No, *I* am sorry. I know you mean well, and I'm glad to see you."

"What happened? I know you were arrested, but I thought you'd be out on bail by now."

Emanuel tugged on a strand of his hair as he talked. "No. The lawyer they gave me was shit, and he didn't get bail."

"Is it Anthony Stone? That's the name Eli gave me."

Emanuel paled. "Anthony Stone?"

"Yes. Isn't that your lawyer?"

"It's my father's lawyer."

"That's good then, right?"

"Nothing is ever good if my father is involved, Dorran. I didn't even know he'd asked Stone to look into this. I don't know why I'm surprised, though. This is exactly something my father would do." He looked around, then leaned toward Dorran. "It was him."

Dorran blinked. "I'm sorry?"

"My father. I know it was him who had Axel killed. It's the only thing that makes sense, especially with his lawyer in the picture now."

What could Dorran say to that? "It looks like he wants to help you. I mean, he sent his lawyer."

Emanuel threw himself back against the chair. "No. My father *never* helps anyone, not even me, not unless he gets something out of it."

Emanuel no doubt knew his father better than Dorran— Dorran didn't even know the man's name—but Dorran couldn't help but wonder if he was being overly dramatic. Why would his father want him to be suspected of murder? And even if he did, why send his lawyer to help Emanuel? That didn't make sense. "What about other suspects? There have to be others who could have done this, right?"

Emanuel shook his head. "I don't know. Axel didn't get along with his wife and her father, but my father makes the most sense."

"His *wife*?"

Emanuel shrugged. "Ex-wife, I guess. They weren't divorced, though, not yet. They were fighting over their kids' custody. I don't know. I didn't ask questions."

Emanuel sounded like he hadn't cared about Axel's kids, and in a way, Dorran could understand it. Emanuel hadn't been serious about his relationship with Axel, and he probably would have broken up with him before he could even meet his children. "Why didn't Axel get along with his wife?"

"I don't know. I think he didn't want to give her what she wanted from the divorce. You'd have to ask her." Emanuel's eyes widened, and he leaned closer again. "Can you do it?"

"Do what?"

"Investigate Axel's death."

Oh, no. Dorran shook his head. "I can't. Eli and his partner are working on it, and I'm not a cop."

"Working on it? I'm in jail, Dorran. That doesn't look like they're working on it. It looks like they've already decided I killed Axel."

"No. I know that's what it feels like, but they're still working on it, I promise."

"Why did they arrest me, then?"

"Because they were pressured to." Eli hadn't said as much, but he'd told Dorran his boss wanted them to get results and that Emanuel was the most obvious suspect. Everything pointed to him, especially the bloody knife. It was true that giving it to Dorran and Eli would have been stupid if he'd been the killer, but that didn't change the fact that a lot of people thought he'd done it anyway.

"Look, I *know* it was my father," Emanuel said. He looked and sounded convinced of that.

"Why do you think that?"

Emanuel looked around again. "My father's name is Jacob Crawford."

Dorran blinked. Everyone knew that name, of course. Jacob Crawford was a real-estate investor and businessman. There was a lot of talk about the fact that he wasn't exactly above board when it came to the stuff he did, and that included having several opponents disappearing when he most needed it. "Your name isn't Crawford."

Emanuel smiled. "Leblanc was my mother's maiden name. I took it when I decided to leave my father."

"But he's still paying your bills."

Emanuel's cheeks flushed. "Yeah."

"Why would he want you to be arrested for murder, Emanuel? I'm not saying he didn't do it. I'm just trying to understand."

"I told you my dad doesn't know I'm gay."

"You did."

"That's why I left. I didn't want him to find out, because I knew he wouldn't take it well. He's a homophobic asshole, and he's never made a secret of it. Racist, too. So I knew that if I wanted to live my life, I'd have to leave."

"And what? You think he found out and decided to kill your boyfriend?" That sounded outlandish no matter how long Dorran thought about it.

"Yes. If he found out, he'd want to make sure I pay for it."

"It's not like he can change the fact that you're gay, though."

"Maybe not, but he can try, and he's never let anything stop him."

"You have to see how this looks, Emanuel. I'm not saying I don't believe you, but I doubt the police will." Eli would probably bust a nut laughing, although considering what Dorran knew about Emanuel's father, it might not be too far from what the man was ready to do.

"I'm telling you, this is what happened. My father wants me to pay for being gay. Then he'll swoop in with his fancy lawyer, and he'll make sure I know that he's helping me only if I agree to do what he wants, which will probably be leaving my art behind and moving back into his mansion, then taking my rightful place as the heir of his businesses. You need to help me, Dorran. Please."

Dorran wanted to say no, especially considering the person he'd be going against if he didn't. How could he, though? He and Emanuel weren't close, hadn't had a chance to grow close, but that didn't change the fact that Emanuel was a friend and that Dorran felt like he had to do what he could to make sure he got out of this situation—and out of jail.

Dorran was still confused and worried when he left the county jail. Emanuel's next step would be an arraignment, and even though Dorran now knew that Emanuel's lawyer was probably an asshole, he hoped the man would manage to get him out. He needed to talk to Eli and check with him whether he and Mel had any other suspects. Maybe Axel's wife? She sounded like she might have something to do with this, but without meeting her, there was no way for Dorran to be sure of that. Besides, Emanuel himself didn't think she'd done it, no matter how angry she was with Axel. It would be easier to ask about her than to mention Emanuel's father to Eli, though. There was no way Eli would buy into Emanuel's theory, even though it might be true. He was probably already investigating Axel's ex-wife, but if she hadn't done anything, that wouldn't help Emanuel. Dorran should probably talk to her, though, just in case Emanuel was wrong.

There was no way Eli would even tell Dorran the ex-wife's name, though. That meant Dorran would have to find her on his own, which was probably better for the sake of his and

Eli's relationship. He didn't think it would be hard. Everyone was on social media now.

Dorran didn't even have to go home to find the ex-wife. He opened the app, found Emanuel's profile, and from there, he found Axel's and his wife's. Once he had her name, it took a bit more work to find out where she lived, but she wasn't too careful about sharing personal stuff, so it wasn't that big of a deal.

Dorran prayed Eli wouldn't use this as the final reason to break up with him and turned on his car.

Axel's ex-wife lived in a nice neighborhood that consisted mostly of houses that all looked similar. The only things that distinguished hers were the bicycles and the toys abandoned in the front yard.

Dorran hated this part. He didn't *want* to talk to Axel's ex-wife. He didn't want to get involved in this investigation. He was sure Eli and Mel had already talked to this woman and that they'd made sure she had an alibi and whatnot. He could probably do without talking to her, but he'd promised Emanuel he would do what he could to find out who had killed Axel. Emanuel might be convinced it was his father, but Dorran wanted to explore the other suspects before turning that way because he doubted Jacob Crawford would want to talk to him.

Dorran took a deep breath and exited his car. He was almost hoping Maggie Ford wouldn't be home, but she opened the door only seconds after he'd knocked. She looked him up and down. "You're not my delivery man."

"Uh, no, I'm not."

"I'm not buying anything."

Dorran forced himself to smile. "That's good, because I'm not selling anything. I wanted to talk to you about your ex-husband, if that's okay with you."

Her expression hardened, and her back straightened. "My

husband. We weren't divorced, no matter what Axel liked to think. What do you want to ask me?"

"Did you know your husband's boyfriend?"

"I know of him, yes."

"And do you think he could have done it?"

Her eyes narrowed. "I'm sorry, who did you say you were?"

"My name is Dorran Wells. I'm Detective Hayes' partner." That wasn't a lie. Dorran *was* Eli's partner, albeit not in the way Maggie Ford probably thought.

"Oh. Well, I already answered your partner's questions when he came the other day."

"I understand. I'm just making sure the Ts are crossed and all that. So, what do you think happened to your husband?"

"I don't know, and honestly, I don't care. Axel was a dick." She snickered. "Or rather, he was *into* dicks."

"Was that the reason you were divorcing?"

She crossed her arms over her chest. "Axel said it wasn't, but I knew better."

"What reason did he give you, then?"

"He said he didn't love me anymore. I told him love isn't all a marriage is made of, but he'd always been a quitter."

"I know you hadn't agreed to the divorce."

"Oh, I didn't mind divorcing him, but I wasn't going to allow him to expose my children to him and his boy toy. That's the only reason we weren't divorced yet. He wanted shared custody, but there was no way I would have said yes to that."

She sounded angry, but not as much as Dorran might have expected from someone who'd killed Axel. His death hadn't been an easy, clean one. Stabbing someone was personal, and Dorran thought the person who'd done was probably one close to Axel, maybe someone who'd acted on impulse.

Or maybe Emanuel was right, and his father had hired a professional killer to make it look like a crime of passion. Why was Dorran doing this again?

A car stopped in the driveway, and Dorran and Maggie both turned to watch an older man hop out of it and amble toward the house. "What's going on, Maggie?" he asked, his gaze on Dorran.

"Nothing. He just wanted to ask a few questions about Axel." She looked at Dorran. "This is my father, Jack Warren."

Warren harrumphed. "Another cop. Goddammit, we already answered all the questions you had. If you want to know what I think, that fag did it, and it's only right that he's behind bars. And Axel deserved it, the little shit. He went looking for trouble, and he found it."

The man certainly didn't have a problem telling Dorran how he felt. "I take it you and Axel didn't get along?"

"Get along? That bastard abandoned my little girl and her babies for a piece of ass. Let me tell you—I don't care if that ass was male or female. He shouldn't even have looked at anyone who wasn't Maggie, and I made sure to tell him that when I found out he wanted a divorce." He wrapped his arm around his daughter's shoulders. "He nearly destroyed my baby, and he got what he deserved. I'm not gonna cry over his death, that's for sure."

Dorran didn't think he'd get much more from those two. They were angry at Axel and while maybe not happy about his death, at the very least relieved and vindicated. "Can you tell me where you both were the night Axel died?" he asked.

That was a mistake. Maggie's father puffed out his chest and glared at Dorran. "What are you implying now?"

"Nothing, sir. Like I told your daughter, I'm just making sure to have every detail."

"We were here," Maggie said.

"Both of you?" Dorran was relieved to be able to talk to her rather than her father. He looked like he might tear off Dorran's head at the first wrong word he let out.

"Yes. Mom died a few years ago, and Dad doesn't live far, so he's usually here in the evening."

"What about at night?" Axel had been killed around midnight, maybe slightly earlier.

"I fell asleep on the couch and woke up the next morning," Maggie's father said. "Neither of us left the house. Do you have what you want?"

Dorran took that as his cue to leave. "Yes, thank you." In truth, he had no idea if he did. He'd thought that maybe Maggie had killed Axel, even though she didn't look shaken, but he wasn't sure. She was angry, yes, but angry enough to stab her husband several times? And even if she had been, why had she taken the knife to Emanuel's place? Did she even know where he lived? And if she did, how had she managed to get in and out without breaking in?

Or maybe it had been Maggie Ford's father. The man seemed to be angry enough at Axel to kill him, and he didn't have an ounce of apology for the way he felt about his son-in-law. He looked like a slumbering man, but he might be faster than Dorran though, and since Axel knew him, he'd probably opened his door without thinking twice about it.

Dorran had more questions than he'd had before talking to the two, and he wasn't sure how to find the answers he needed.

Eli was waiting for Dorran when Dorran got home. Dorran hadn't expected it, and he found himself speechless, no doubt because he'd just done something that he knew would piss Eli off when he found out about it — and Dorran didn't doubt he would. Eli *always* found out when Dorran stuck his nose where he shouldn't.

"Hey," he said, closing the apartment door.

Eli didn't get up from the couch, but he did smile. "Hey. Where were you?"

"Out."

Eli rolled his eyes. "I noticed that. Good thing you gave me a key."

"Yeah."

"So, I don't know if you've already thought about dinner, but I thought we could order in and eat on the couch? I have no intention of cooking anything, although you're welcome to cook if you'd rather do that."

Dorran wrinkled his nose. He didn't like to cook, and he did so only because he had to feed himself and it was cheaper and no doubt better for his health than takeout. He wished he could get away with that, though. "I guess I *could* defrost some soup or something."

"Or we could order from that Thai place you like."

Dorran's stomach rumbled at the thought of Pad Thai. "Or we could do that, yes."

Eli grinned. "Good thing I already placed an order, then."

Dorran laughed. "And that you know me well enough to realize I wouldn't want frozen soup for dinner. Why don't you keep on relaxing on the couch? I'm just going to go wash up and change." There was no way Dorran would eat Pad Thai with his jeans on. That deserved an elastic waistband.

They were well into their takeout containers when Eli asked, "So, what did you find out today?"

Dorran blinked, the taste of lime and tamarind in his mouth was making it hard to think. "What do you mean?"

"You went to see Emanuel, didn't you?"

Dorran swallowed. He cleaned his mouth with his napkin, stalling for time as he tried to think about his answer. Should he deny it? But Eli wouldn't have a problem finding out he was lying if he did. Hell, he probably wouldn't have brought this up if he wasn't already a hundred percent sure Dorran had seen Emanuel. "He says it was his father."

Eli nodded. "That's what he told us, too, and honestly,

considering who his father his, I'm inclined to believe him."

Dorran blinked. That wasn't what he'd expected, not from Eli. "You do?"

"The man has a bad reputation, and not only because his rivals keep disappearing. I've always thought he was dirty, and it's obvious he won't stop for anything to get what he wants. Killing his son's boyfriend is probably nothing next to some of the other stuff he's done."

"Isn't it a bit out there, though? I mean, Emanuel told me his father is homophobic, and from what I know, he's also controlling, but killing Emanuel's boyfriend? And making it look like Emanuel did it? That sounds like it should be in a book, and I'm pretty sure the reviews would say it's too out-landish to be believable."

"Maybe. I'm not sure of anything right now, to be honest."

"Yet you arrested Emanuel."

Eli put down his container. "Because I had to. I couldn't ignore the proof, not when it's as big as a bloody knife. That doesn't mean I'm not still looking into it."

"I know." Dorran bit his lower lip. He should be honest now rather than wait for Eli to find out what he'd done and explode. "I found Axel's ex-wife today."

Eli stared. "By found, you mean you looked for her?"

"Yes. Emanuel mentioned her and her father a few times, and I thought I'd go talk to them and see what they had to say."

Eli sighed. "You talked to them."

"Yes."

"And they told you what, exactly?"

"Uh, that they were both home when Axel was killed. That they weren't sorry he was dead and that he'd deserved it for the way he left Maggie."

"That's pretty much what Mel and I got from them. Why did they talk to you?"

Dorran looked down. "I might have told them I was your partner. I didn't lie, exactly, but I also didn't tell them the entire truth."

"You sure didn't. Let's hope they don't realize what happened. You should stay away from them for now, Dorran."

Dorran frowned and looked at Eli again. "You're not angry?"

Eli shrugged. "Nah. I knew you were going to stick your nose into this. Emanuel is your friend, and with the way you went looking for Francis' murderer when you didn't even know him, I'm not surprised you're ready to do this for a neighbor you like."

Dorran peered at Eli. He didn't look angry. There was a glint of irritation in his eyes, but Dorran was surprised that was the only indication he wasn't happy. "Are you going to tell me to stay away from your case?"

"Are you going to listen if I do?"

Dorran didn't answer, but he didn't have to because Eli continued.

"That's what I thought. I need you to be careful, Dorran. You've already been shot and assaulted. I don't want to lose you. And if you're not careful, I might have to arrest you."

Dorran wiggled his eyebrows. "We haven't used your handcuffs yet."

Eli smiled, but he was serious when he said, "I'm not joking, Dorran, I get what you're trying to do. You wouldn't be you if you didn't try to help the people who need it. It's one of the reasons I love you. I don't want to lose you to it, though. You *have* to be careful, especially with Jacob Crawford in the mix. You can't just go talk to him."

"I doubt he'd even let me into the building."

"And that's a good thing. He's a dangerous man."

"I know. We have to help Emanuel, though. He doesn't deserve to spend the rest of his life in jail because his father is a controlling asshole."

"He doesn't, but you need to let me take care of this. It's my job. I promise I'll dig deeper and that I'll keep Emanuel's words in mind, but I won't be able to focus on my work if I worry about you."

Dorran sighed. He knew Eli was right, no matter how little he liked to admit it. "I can't promise I won't poke around a bit."

"As long as you stay away from Crawford, I'm okay with that."

It was more than Dorran had expected he'd get. He put down his container and swung his leg over Eli's thighs, straddling him. Eli's smile was surprised but pleased as Dorran settled there, and he grabbed Dorran's hips. "We seem to be making love on the couch more than in the bed lately," he murmured as he leaned forward to kiss Dorran's neck.

"We can do it here *and* there."

Eli chuckled. "I doubt I'll be up for going twice tonight, but we can certainly try."

And to Dorran's delight and pleasure, they did.

CHAPTER EIGHT

It hadn't been hard to find Anthony Stone's phone number. Dorran hadn't even had to ask Eli.

The lawyer was one of the associates in one of the best-known firms in the city. Dorran had no idea what that meant precisely, except that it was clear from his picture on the website that the man earned a substantial paycheck. His hairstyle had to cost as much as all the clothes in Dorran's closet put together—although, of course, Dorran usually wore pajamas at work, so it didn't mean much.

Getting to Stone was another matter. An assistant answered when he called the number he'd found on the firm's website. At first, she refused to put Dorran through, and he had to use Emanuel's name. He didn't know if she'd finally agreed because he'd said he was one of Emanuel's closest friends or because she suspected he'd call again and again until he finally got to Stone, but he didn't care.

He was about to talk to Emanuel's lawyer.

"Stone."

Dorran blinked at the harshness of the man's voice. "Hello, my name is Dorran Wells."

"I know. My secretary told me. What do you want?"

This wasn't going as well as Dorran had hoped it would. "I'd like to talk to you about Emanuel. Uh, Emanuel Leblanc. I know you're his lawyer."

"You're right, I am, and I don't understand why you thought I'd talk to you about him. Are you a reporter? A cop?"

"No. I'm a friend of Emanuel's. His neighbor, actually. I was just wondering what you were doing to get him out of jail."

"That's my job to decide, isn't it? Thank you for calling, Mr. Mells, but I'm not sure why you did. Please don't bother calling again."

Dorran was left blinking at the screen of his phone when Stone hung up. "*Mr. Mells?* What the fuck?" Anthony Stone was a rude asshole, and Dorran hoped he was more respectful when he was in a courtroom, because otherwise, Emanuel didn't stand a chance.

He sighed and put the phone on the couch next to him. He wasn't sure what else he could do for Emanuel. He'd talked to Axel's wife and her father. He'd tried to talk to the lawyer his father had hired for him. That was it. There was no one else to talk to, nothing else to do as far as Dorran could see.

Except that wasn't true, was it? Dorran had an ability most people didn't have. He could see people who'd died, including Axel. Getting answers from him might be useless since he wouldn't be able to use it to free Emanuel since he wouldn't have any proof, but it could be a start to *find* proof. If Axel could tell Dorran who had killed him, Dorran could try to find a way to let the police know, possibly a way that didn't involve Eli. Maybe an anonymous phone call?

But he wouldn't be able to do anything until he found out more. That meant he had to contact Axel and make him talk this time. Maybe Francis could help him.

Dorran crossed his legs and closed his eyes. It was easier to meditate now that he was regularly training, but it was still harder than when Carole was there to guide him. He was lucky he and Francis were close, because asking him to come usually worked, and not because Dorran was good at this. He felt like he'd barely started to understand what he was supposed to do. He certainly needed to study a lot more if he ever wanted to get to Carole's level.

"Dorran."

Dorran smiled and opened his eyes. Francis was sitting on the edge of the coffee table, his hands propping him up behind him, his legs crossed at the ankles. He looked entirely comfortable and as if he belonged there, which he did, kind of. There were still traces of him in the apartment, since it hadn't been empty when Dorran moved in. Once he'd realized the ghost haunting him was Francis, he'd decided to keep some of his things to make him feel welcome.

He hoped he'd succeeded.

"Hey, Francis."

Francis grinned. "Let me guess. You want to talk to Axel, and you need my help to do it."

That made Dorran feel guilty. "It's also nice to have you around. When you don't pinch my ass, anyway."

Francis laughed. "Don't worry about it, Dorran. I understand that you're focused on what happened and on trying to find a way to get our Emanuel out of jail. I want him to come home, too, and if I have to get to work for that to happen, I'm all for it."

Dorran nodded. "Do you think you can talk to Axel? I'd try, but I'm pretty sure it hasn't been long enough. It took me months to manage to hear you, and you'd been dead for a bit before I even realized you existed. Axel's death is a lot more recent."

"It is, and unless I'm wrong, he's probably still freaking out over being dead." Francis tsked. "Those youngsters."

Francis had been sixty-two when he'd died. Dorran didn't know how healthy he'd been except for his diabetes, but he looked good now—although of course, he was dead. "It couldn't have been easy when *you* died."

"No, but I didn't have an older ghost to guide me."

"You can't tell me no one else died in this building."

Francis' nephew had, but since he was the one who'd killed Francis, Dorran doubted Francis had wanted to talk to him.

Francis waved. "Of course people died, but most of them crossed over. It was their time. It *wasn't* mine, though, and I wasn't ready to let go of my apartment and my things." He paused and looked at Dorran. "I'm glad you got them, you know."

Dorran reached for Francis on instinct, but of course, his hand went right through Francis'. It wasn't cold or anything, just weird.

Dorran dropped his hand to his lap. "What do you think, then? Can you talk to him? Emanuel is convinced his father hired someone to kill Axel and put the blame on him. It would be useful to know if it was someone Axel didn't know." If anything, Dorran wouldn't have to talk to Axel's ex-wife again. He hadn't minded her, but her father wasn't the nicest person.

"I can try. I can't promise he'll answer me, though."

"That's okay. It's more than I have right now."

Dorran's phone rang, and he looked down, smiling when he saw it was Charlie. He looked up again, but Francis was gone. Hopefully, he went to find Axel and ask him what had happened to him.

"Charlie, man. I was starting to think you'd forgotten about me now that you live with Theresa and everything. I know I can't compare to her, but I thought I meant something to you." Dorran sniffed dramatically, but he was smiling like an idiot.

"Oh, fuck off, Dorran. You're no better than me. Still doing the horizontal dance with that cop of yours?"

Dorran groaned. "You can't call it that. Come on, Charlie. You're thirty, not sixty." And even Francis didn't call sex the horizontal dance. Not that he and Dorran talked about sex, of course. That would be like talking about sex with his father, and it wasn't something Dorran could imagine doing.

"What are you doing tonight?" There was still laughter in Charlie's voice, and Dorran's heart squeezed at the sound. He missed his best friend, more than he'd thought possible, especially considering all the shit he was going through right now.

"I don't know. Eli hasn't told me when he thinks he'll be home from work."

"*Home* from work, huh? You two are that close already?"

Damn. Charlie didn't know about the problems Dorran and Eli were having. "Kind of. I'll tell you tonight at dinner?"

"That works for me. Do you want me to come to your side of town, or are you coming here?"

They didn't live far away from each other. "Halfway through? There's that nice little sushi place."

"Still eating raw fish, huh?"

"Same goes for you?"

"Yep. Theresa hates sushi, so it'll be a treat. Seven tonight?"

"Perfect." Dorran would have to text Eli to let him know he wouldn't be home, just in case Eli decided to come around like he'd done the other day. He'd know that Dorran wouldn't mind if he did come in to wait for him, but at least he wouldn't be waiting. "See you tonight, Charlie." It would be good for Dorran to forget about this case for a little while.

He couldn't wait.

Dorran was smiling even before he walked into the sushi restaurant. His smile widened when he noticed Charlie was already there, sitting in a corner pouring over the menu, his red hair all over the place as if he'd been running his hands through it.

It was good to see him. It was good to be able to forget about Emanuel, ghosts, and even Eli for a little bit and focus on someone Dorran didn't have to fight for or with.

"You're late," Charlie said when Dorran sat down in the chair in front of him. He was smiling, too, and they probably looked like two idiots.

"Sorry. I had to go back because I forgot my phone."

Charlie rolled his eyes. "Of course you did. Say what you want, but this was easier when we lived together."

"It was, but I wasn't enthusiastic about the sex noises once you met Theresa."

Charlie's cheeks flushed, and he kicked Dorran under the table. Dorran laughed. He could feel himself relax, and damn, he needed it.

They chatted about something or other while they decided what to eat and ordered, but Charlie pounced as soon as the waitress had turned her back on them. "What's going on?"

Dorran didn't want to do this. "Nothing. We're having sushi. We're talking."

"Bullshit, and you know it. I don't have to live with you to know something is up. Now, you can tell me of your own free will, or I can sic Theresa on you and wait until she gets the answers I want."

"Should I be scared?"

"Very much so. You know her. She won't stop until she has everything she wants, and that's never a pleasant experience. Trust me on that."

Maybe it was a good thing that she wasn't there tonight. Dorran sighed. "Where do you want me to start?"

Charlie grimaced. "That bad?"

"You have no idea."

Charlie looked around and leaned closer to the table. His tie ended up in his glass, and Dorran was grateful for the short moment of reprieve. He should have known better than to think Charlie wouldn't notice his life was a mess. He knew Charlie would back off if he didn't want to talk about it, but he'd worry, and that was the last thing Dorran wanted. Charlie needed to focus on Theresa, not to obsess over him and his well-being. "Is it your *housemate*?" Charlie asked in a loud whisper.

Dorran rolled his eyes. "You're not as discreet as you think. And no, it's not Francis, not entirely. Emanuel was arrested for stabbing his boyfriend to death, though."

The waitress had been coming their way with Dorran's drink, and she froze at his words. Dorran cocked his head at her, smiling when she finally put down his glass. She scurried away.

"Way to make friends, Dorran," Charlie teased.

"I'm not here to make friends."

"So your neighbor was arrested for murder? The one with the long hair?"

"Yes, him."

"I wouldn't have thought he could kill someone, not from looking at him. Of course, that doesn't mean anything."

"I don't think he did it, though. Eli and Mel arrested him because they had to and because the evidence points to him, but there's no way he had anything to do with it."

"You're going to have to explain."

Dorran didn't want to, but Charlie was intrigued now, and he'd keep asking questions. Dorran told him what had happened with the knife and what Eli had told him about the case. Charlie's eyes widened as Dorran spoke, especially when he got to the bit where he'd managed to see Axel's ghost.

"You talked to him?" Charlie asked.

"Not really. He hasn't been . . . *asleep* long," Dorran said since the waitress was coming their way with their meal. "He doesn't understand what's going on, you know? But I tried."

"What about Francis? He helped you with your brother's girlfriend, didn't he?"

"He's trying, and now that I can talk to him, it's easier, but he hasn't had any more success than me. Axel is freaking out, and so is Emanuel, and I'm not sure what I can do for either of them."

"Have you contacted that lady you told me about?"

Charlie had never been anything but accepting when it came to Dorran's new quirk of seeing ghosts. "I've been working with her." Dorran smiled at the waitress when she put his plate in front of him. "But it's hard. And Eli, well, let's just say he doesn't like Carole and what she does much."

Charlie waited until the waitress was gone to ask for more details. "What do you mean, he doesn't like what she does?" he asked, waving his chopsticks around.

"He knows what I can do, and he's seen Francis himself, but he likes to pretend it didn't happen and he freaks out every time I bring it up or when he finds Carole working with me."

"Well, he's jaded. He has to be, with his job. It's probably not easy for him to metabolize the fact that ghosts exist and that his boyfriend can see them."

"I understand that, but it's putting even more strain on our relationship, and I'm not sure what to do about it. It's not something I can turn off, you know? I asked Carole about it, and she says that if I ignore it, it's going to get to the point where I can't control it, and the . . . *sleepers* will swamp me and never leave me alone. It seems they can get overly enthusiastic when they finally find someone who can communicate with them, especially if they've been *asleep* for a while."

"So there's no going around it or ignoring it."

"No." And Eli was going to have to accept that if he wanted to be with Dorran.

"Have you talked to Eli about this? I mean, he loves you. Surely he understands there's nothing you can do."

Dorran rubbed his forehead. "I don't know. He knows about this, of course, but he's resistant. Maybe if this was the only thing wrong between us, we could make it work, but it's not."

"Are you and Eli breaking up, Dorran?" Charlie's voice was gentle, but hearing him say that broke Dorran's heart.

"I don't know. I don't want to, and I don't think he wants it, either."

"Then what's the problem?"

Dorran put down his chopsticks. "You know why I broke up with him the first time around, right?"

"Because he didn't want to come out and you were done hiding."

"He's out now, or at least, he told his family he's gay, and he's not hiding it at work. But he's still hiding me."

"Not from his colleagues, right? I remember his partner."

"From his family. They might know he's gay, but they haven't accepted it, especially his mother. She's been pushing him to date women, introducing him to her friends' daughters, things like that. And when she asked him if he was coming to Sunday lunch alone, he told her he wasn't seeing anyone."

Charlie grimaced. "In front of you?"

"Yes. I understand he needs time. Families can be a mess. I know all about that. I'm not asking to meet them tomorrow, just that he stop behaving as if I'm not part of his life."

Charlie leaned back in his chair. "The way I see it, you have two options. Either you accept that it's going to take him some time to deal with this and you stay in the part of his life he hides, or you break up with him. I doubt giving him an ultimatum will work, not knowing him, but I can understand why being pushed back in the closet hurts."

"It's not exactly in the closet. I mean, he's only hiding me from his family, not the fact that he's gay. They already know that."

"And they're a huge part of his life. Yes, it's hard to deal with them, but Eli is letting them walk all over him. They already know he's gay. The fact that they can't accept it is their problem, not yours. You either have to deal with that or get out, Dorran." He reached over the table and grabbed Dorran's hand. "I know you love him. I know you want to be with him. You have to decide if you can stand the pain of listening to him tell his family you don't exist. You have to decide if he and your relationship are worth it."

How was Dorran supposed to do that?

CHAPTER NINE

Dorran didn't have any more answers to that question than he had before, even though a few days had passed. He'd seen Charlie again for coffee, but Charlie hadn't pushed or asked what was going on, and Dorran's thoughts were still confused.

This was why he didn't like relationships. Eli had the power to tear Dorran's heart out of his chest and crush it — because Dorran had given that power to him. Because he'd fallen in love with Eli all over again.

He wasn't sure he could get over it, that he could push his feelings away. He didn't want to be miserable, though, and he knew that was what would happen if he didn't do *something*. *What* could he do, though? Charlie was right — either Dorran broke up with Eli, or he stayed with him and powered through being hidden from his family.

He hated both those options.

Dorran's phone rang as he walked out of the elevator on his floor. He wasn't sure he wanted to answer when he saw Eli's picture on the screen, but ignoring him would probably freak him out, and the last thing Dorran needed was to have his boyfriend barge into his apartment to save him.

"Yes?"

"Dorran. I thought you'd want to know — Emanuel was released."

Dorran stopped in the middle of the hallway. "*What?* But the judge didn't even allow him to get out on bail."

"I know. His lawyer was apparently able to convince the

judge that Mel and I aren't doing our jobs correctly and that instead of investigating the murder, we kicked his ass into jail and decided that was good enough for us."

"And the judge believed him? Even with the bloody knife?"

"Looks like he did. Some of the evidence points that way."

Dorran was torn between feeling sorry for Eli and angry on his behalf about the insinuation that he wasn't good at his job, and relieved that Emanuel was out of jail. It would give them time to find a way to keep him out, although Dorran had no idea how they would do that. "I'm sorry."

Eli chuckled. "No, you're not. You got what you wanted. Your friend is free."

"Maybe, but I hate that someone is saying you're not good at your job."

"It's the way it is, Dorran. Don't worry about me. Besides, the only reason Mel and I arrested Emanuel was that we were pressured into it. I can't say I'm sorry I'll have more time to investigate this."

"You don't think he did it." Eli hadn't said it out loud, but Dorran knew it.

"I don't know for sure, but you weren't wrong when you said that anyone with a brain wouldn't have brought you the knife, not when they knew I could be there. It would have been much easier to throw it away and act surprised once someone came to tell him his boyfriend was dead. It was the knife that pushed us to arrest Emanuel, and I'm pretty sure his lawyer is working on having that proof dismissed or something." Eli sighed. "But anyway, this means that I don't know when I'll leave work today. Mel and I are going over everything again, so it's going to take a while."

"You can come whenever you want, even if I'm asleep. I don't mind."

"I don't know. Maybe I should go home. I need to feed the

cat anyway, and to grab some clean clothes. I'll text you later, though."

Things would be much easier if they lived together, but Dorran didn't say it. It wasn't the right time, not when their relationship felt so fragile and brittle. "All right."

Dorran got his keys out of his pocket, his phone still in his hand even though Eli had hung up.

The door swung open, and someone grabbed Dorran. He saw a flash of something—someone—as he was pulled forward and slammed against the wall face first.

"You need to stay away from Emanuel Leblanc," a voice growled into his ear.

"I—what?"

Questioning the man assaulting him probably wasn't the best idea. The man pulled Dorran back, then slammed him against the wall again. Dorran's entire face hurt, and he was pretty sure his cheek was scraped.

"Stay. Away. From Emanuel Leblanc. I won't be this nice next time."

Shit. If this was the guy being nice, Dorran didn't want to be in the same room as him when he was angry.

He kept his mouth shut because even he realized it was the best way out of this. The man pushed him one last time, then released him. Dorran stayed right where he was slumped against the wall and listened to the man leave. The door clicked closed, and Dorran turned around, then slid down the wall until his ass was on the floor.

Blood pulsed in his cheek, and his eye felt like it was swelling. His lower lip was split down the middle. His face hurt, and he knew he needed to get up and go clean up.

Eli was going to shit kittens when he saw him.

Dorran hoped Eli would go home tonight like he'd said, even though it would only delay the inevitable—so of course, he decided to come around anyway, and he even managed to get to Dorran's apartment early enough that he found Dorran still on the couch watching TV.

Dorran tensed at the sound of a key in his front door. He knew it was Eli—and that Eli wasn't going to be happy. His lip and eye had swollen, and there were scrapes on his cheek. There was no way he could hide it from Eli, so he didn't even try to.

"Hey. I wasn't sure you'd still be awake," Eli said as he walked in. He closed the door behind himself and looked a Dorran.

The smile on his lips died when he saw Dorran's face. "What happened?" he asked, rushing to Dorran's side.

Dorran shook his head. "Nothing."

"Bullshit, Dorran." Eli knelt by the couch and gently cupped Dorran's good cheek. "Tell me whose ass I have to kick."

Dorran sighed. "I don't know. Someone was in my apartment when I came back. I don't know how they got in, because the door was locked. The guy slammed me against the wall a few times and told me to stay away from the investigation on Axel's murder." That wasn't exactly the truth, but Dorran knew what would happen if he told Eli the man had warned him about staying away from Emanuel. He'd have Dorran moved out of the building faster than Dorran could take in the breath to protest, and it wasn't something Dorran could deal with right now.

"Then you need to stay away. And why didn't you call me, Dorran? Did you go to the ER?"

"I didn't need the ER. It's just a split lip and a few—"

"Dorran. You can't do this. You can't keep something like this to yourself. You could have been seriously hurt."

"But I wasn't." And he was going to double-check that his door was locked when he left the apartment from now on.

"Dammit, Dorran. We're together, right? We're a couple, a

team. I don't care if you hurt your pinky toe by slamming it against the coffee table. You *need* to tell me this kind of thing."

Dorran narrowed his eyes. He was tired and in pain, and he hated how protective Eli was, because he made it sound like Dorran wasn't able to do anything on his own. And maybe he wasn't—he should probably start taking self-defense lessons if people were going to keep on assaulting him and shooting at him—but that didn't mean Eli should mother him the way he was trying to. "Are you sure of that?" he snapped. He shouldn't have said those words, though. He didn't want to fight, and that was precisely what would happen if Dorran pushed.

Eli frowned. "What do you mean?"

Dorran sighed. "Nothing. I'm just tired."

"What do you mean, Dorran?"

There were going to do this. *Shit.* "Are we really a team, Eli? I know you're trying to juggle our relationship and your family, and I get how hard it is, I do. I'm just not sure I can do this again."

Eli took his hand away from Dorran's cheek. "What?"

"I love you. I think I always have. But sometimes, love isn't enough." Dorran hadn't let himself think about this, but he'd known things were going to go this way since the beginning. "I don't want to break up with you a second time, and I don't want to force you to face your family head-on, but I can't be a secret. If you don't think that eventually, you'll be able to tell your parents about me, then . . ." There was nothing more to say. Dorran didn't have to lay it all out. Eli knew what he was talking about.

Eli got up. "I can't do this right now."

That was more than fine with Dorran. "All right. Just think about it, please. This isn't an ultimatum. It's just me saying that if you don't think you can deal with telling your parents about me, ever, then maybe you shouldn't." *And maybe we shouldn't be together.*

Dorran wasn't surprised that Eli left. He would have left, too, if he could have. But instead, he snuggled deeper into the couch and tried to ignore the tears prickling his eyes.

CHAPTER TEN

Dorran was going crazy. He'd been trying to focus on his work for the past few days, but he couldn't.

Emanuel was home. He hadn't come to see Dorran, and Dorran hadn't gone to see him. He couldn't forget what the man who'd assaulted him had said, no matter how much he hated it. He didn't like not being a good friend, but he had no idea what would happen if he went to talk to Emanuel, so it was probably more advisable to stay in his apartment.

He needed to do something, though. He couldn't just stay there while Emanuel's life went down the drain.

Not that he knew what was happening with the case. Eli hadn't so much as texted him since he'd left after their argument. Dorran hoped that meant he was still thinking about it rather than that he'd decided to stay away from him.

So Dorran was going crazy. He hadn't left his apartment yet, and he couldn't stop thinking about Eli and Emanuel. He doubted anything he could do or say would make Eli come back to him, so he decided to focus on Emanuel, even though it would probably end badly for him and his face.

The guy had told him to stay away from Emanuel, but not from the case, which was why Dorran decided to talk to Axel's ex-wife again. He doubted he'd get anything from her, but it would be something to do other than stare at the wall in his apartment and mope around.

He looked at himself in his rearview mirror and grimaced. He hoped Mrs. Ford wouldn't say anything about his face, and that she wouldn't realize he wasn't an officer of the law.

She had.

She took one look at him when she opened the door, and her expression changed. "What the fuck do you want?"

"I just wanted to ask you if you'd remembered anything else about your husband."

"Don't think I don't know you faked being a police officer."

"I didn't. I told you I was Detective Hayes' partner, and I am. I'm his *life* partner." Hopefully for a long time, although Dorran wouldn't have sworn on that right now.

Maggie Ford slammed her front door in his face.

Dorran sighed. It wasn't like he'd expected anything anyway, but he was still disappointed. There *had* to be a way to prove Emanuel's father was behind this wasn't there? Dorran had pretty much accepted he was, but not even Emanuel could find out more.

Unless he could? Maybe Dorran should talk to him. He didn't think the man who'd attacked him was hanging around their building spying on them, so he'd probably be safe even if he went to talk to Emanuel.

Dorran slid into his car and almost screamed when he saw that Axel was sitting in the passenger seat. He managed not to, and hopefully, to behave as if everything were normal and there wasn't a ghost sitting in his car with him.

"Hello, Axel," he said. Would Axel be able to understand and answer him this time around?

Axel was staring at the house where his wife and their two children lived. Dorran sighed. This was no doubt bringing up a lot of memories for Axel, and while he didn't want to interrupt, he needed to get out of there before Maggie Ford called the cops on him.

"I'm sorry you were killed, Axel. I'm sure your children will be okay, though. They'll be hurt that their father is dead, but they're in good hands." Maggie hadn't sounded like a good wife, but then, Axel probably hadn't been a good husband, either. Those were different from being good parents, though.

Dorran turned the car on. "Can you tell me anything about the person who killed you? I know it wasn't Emanuel, but I don't have proof, and he might go to jail again if I don't find anything." Dorran wished he could meditate to get closer to Axel, but he was driving, so that was out. He did try to empty his mind and focus on Axel and the road in front of him, though. He blocked out everything else except for every thought about Emanuel and Eli.

"I didn't know him."

Dorran almost jerked the car to the side of the road at the whisper coming from Axel. "Are you sure?"

"I am. I'd never seen him. He hurt me."

"I know, and I'm sorry. Can you maybe identify him? Or tell me what he looked like?"

Axel shook his head.

Dorran doubted he'd have managed anyway, because he was already fading.

Dorran did stop once Axel was gone entirely. He parked on the side of the road and closed his eyes, pressing his forehead against the steering wheel.

What the fuck was he going to do? His relationship was a mess—if he even still had one—he had no idea how to help Emanuel, and someone was probably watching him and waiting to attack him again.

His life was a mess, and he had no idea how to solve it.

Dorran was extra careful when he opened his apartment door. He suspected he was going to be for a while after what had happened the last time he hadn't been.

The apartment was empty, though. Sunlight streamed through the windows, illuminating it enough that Dorran was sure of it. The bedrooms doors were open, but unless his attacker was in one of the bathrooms, Dorran was alone in his home. He still made a quick round, just to be sure.

A knock on the door interrupted him, and he rushed to open it, thinking—hoping—it might be Eli.

It wasn't.

Emanuel stood there, biting his lower lip, his hair neatly tied back from his face. Dorran grinned at him. "It's good to see you."

Emanuel smiled. "It's good not to be behind bars anymore. Can I come in?"

"Of course." Dorran stepped to the side to let him pass. "I'm sorry I didn't come to visit you."

"It's fine. What happened to your face? Is that why you didn't come?" Emanuel frowned. "It wasn't your boyfriend, was it?"

Dorran's brows shot up. "Of course not. Eli would never hurt me."

"Isn't that what they all say?"

"He wouldn't, Emanuel. Are you okay? Did something happen while you were in jail?"

Emanuel flopped onto the couch. "No. I'm okay, or as okay as I can be, I guess."

Dorran sat next to him. "Want to talk about it?"

"Not really, but I guess I should do it while I can."

"You won't be arrested again." Or at least Dorran hoped he wouldn't be. He *knew* Emanuel hadn't done anything. "Your lawyer is good, right? Rude, but good. I mean, I went to the firm's website, and it looks like your father dropped a lot of money when he hired him."

"Anthony Stone is outstanding. I doubt I'll ever see the inside of a jail again." Emanuel's smile faded. "That's not what I meant. Getting me out of there came with compromises."

Dorran should have expected that. Emanuel had warned him about it. "Your father?"

"Yes." Emanuel rubbed his face with both his hands. "He told me to come back home."

"Told you?"

Emanuel's laughter was humorless. "Yeah. He doesn't ask. He orders, and that's what he did. He ordered me to go home. That was the compromise. I got out of jail only to end up in a new, golden one."

"You don't have to go. I know your father has been paying your bills and everything, but I'm sure you can find a way to make it without his money. I'll help you."

Emanuel shook his head. "It's not that. I make enough money with my art to be able to survive. But my father's lawyer is only going to represent me if I do what my father wants. My father didn't say it outright, but I think he'll also make sure that this time, the murder accusation sticks. You know he was the one who had the knife put in my apartment. Who's to say he wouldn't manage to plant more proof that I killed Axel? I can't risk it, Dorran."

Dorran raked a hand through his hair, wincing when he pulled at his still sensitive eye. "Is there any way we can prove you didn't do it?"

"I don't know. Stone told me the reason I was let go was that there was a print on the knife that wasn't mine."

That caught Dorran's attention. "A print?" Eli hadn't told him that. Of course, Eli hadn't told him anything since they'd fought the day he was assaulted.

"I don't know anything else, just that this is how Stone managed to get me out."

That made sense. If there was a print on the knife, it gave the cops another suspect. "Do you know who the print belongs to?"

"I have no idea. Stone didn't tell me anything else, well, unless you count his threat to let me rot in jail."

"But if there was a print, that means Eli and Mel can find

the real killer. You won't go back to jail, no matter what your father is saying."

Emanuel looked desperate. "But don't you see, Dorran? My father will do *anything* to get me back. He — he found out that I'm gay. That's why he had Axel killed."

Dorran swallowed. He couldn't believe someone would do that. Kill your son's boyfriend, a father, just because your son was dating him? Emanuel wasn't even in love with Axel. "What was he trying to do? It's not like you won't ever have another boyfriend."

"Not if my father has a say in it, and as of now, he does. I can't risk it. I can't risk my life or someone else's."

"He'd kill others?"

Emanuel's smile was sad. "Yeah, he would. You don't know him, Dorran, and I hope you never do."

Dorran suspected that he'd met the killer, though, or at the very least, one of Emanuel's father's men. He hadn't told Emanuel how he'd gotten hurt, and he wasn't going to. Emanuel had enough on his plate right now.

"I don't know what to do, Dorran."

Dorran didn't, either.

"Can you ask Eli who the print belonged to?" Emanuel asked. "Maybe they could arrest the guy, and my father really wouldn't be able to use this to threaten me."

Dorran bit his lower lip. "Eli and I have been fighting."

"Oh, Dorran. Again?"

"Yeah. I haven't heard from him in a few days, and I don't want to call him just to ask him about this."

"Of course. I wouldn't ask that of you." Emanuel hesitated. "Do you think you're going to break up with him?"

"I have no idea. I don't want to, but I also don't want Eli to hide me from his family." Dorran didn't want to talk about Eli, though. "If we manage to make sure everyone knows you're innocent, what will your father do? Do you really think he'll kill someone else?"

"That, or he'll find a way to manipulate me in some other way. He always gets what he wants, Dorran. Always. That's never going to change, and he doesn't care what he has to do to make sure I obey him. He's dangerous."

Dorran understood that, but he knew there had to be a way to keep the man off Emanuel's back. He didn't appear to love his son. He wanted to control Emanuel, no doubt like he controlled every other aspect of his life.

He hadn't counted on Dorran, though. Dorran wasn't sure what he could do, but he'd find a way to keep Emanuel out of his father's hands.

There had to be one.

CHAPTER ELEVEN

There had to be a way to get Emanuel's father to back off, but if there was, Dorran hadn't found it yet. It wasn't that he hadn't thought about it—he hadn't *stopped* asking himself what to do ever since Emanuel had left his apartment yesterday. He didn't have anything better to do anyway, and he wanted to help. It was better than to obsess over Eli and the reason he hadn't called yet.

So what could Dorran do?

"You could kill him."

Dorran glared at Francis. The ghost hadn't been around in the past several days, and when he'd arrived earlier and seen Dorran's face, he'd vowed not to leave Dorran's apartment again. No matter how many times Dorran had tried to make him see that it wasn't like he could do anything even if he was there if Dorran was assaulted again, he hadn't budged. He'd stuck by Dorran's side since last night, including when Dorran had taken a shower—even though Dorran had told him to leave him alone. He might have suspected Francis wanted to get a peek if he hadn't seen how worried Francis really was.

"What?" Francis asked. He was sitting on the couch, his long legs stretched in front of him, crossed at the ankle. He looked real, so much so that Dorran could almost imagine touching him if he reached out.

He didn't. "We can't kill Emanuel's father."

"Why not?"

"Because I'm not a killer, for one."

"Then hire one like he did."

"With what money, Francis?"

Francis pouted. "I wish I'd known you before. I'd have left you everything I had."

This was where Dorran would normally reach over and pat Francis' knee. He couldn't, not unless he wanted to end up patting the couch. "I can't kill the guy, no matter how much I wish I could."

"You think he sent the asshole who hurt you?"

"Probably." Dorran wouldn't have told anyone else, but Francis couldn't protect him, even though he'd probably try.

"Yet you're still sticking your nose into this. Eli isn't wrong when he says you don't think things through, you know."

"Is that what you think? That I should rethink telling him I'm not sure I can be with him?"

Francis' expression twisted. "No. I think that if you really don't think you can do it, then you did the right thing."

"But?"

"But you have to be sure. As much as I don't like Eli sometimes, he's good for you, and he's a good man, too. You can be happy with him."

"But I have to let him hide me from his family."

Francis linked his fingers together on his stomach. "Is it that important? I mean, are you going to go with him to Sunday lunch soon? Do you want to become his family's friend?"

"No." They were nice enough when he was a teenager, but now that he knew how they'd reacted to Eli being gay, Dorran wasn't sure he wanted to have much contact with them.

"Then what's the problem? You think Eli is going to cheat on you with one of the women his mother keeps pushing toward him?"

"Of course not." Eli wasn't a cheater. He'd never been.

"Then again, what is the problem? You don't want to spend time with his family? I get that it's hurtful when he says he's not dating anyone, but you know the truth. He loves you.

He's also afraid to lose his family, though. He already came out to them, and it had to be hard enough. Coming out a second time sounds like hell."

"Now you're making me feel like shit," Dorran grumbled.

"That's not what I was trying to do. I'm just saying give him a chance. He knows how to deal with them. Better than you do, and since it's not important to you that they know, well . . ." Francis shrugged. "Just be very sure of what you want and what you're doing, is all I'm saying."

The sound of a key in the front door lock made Dorran jump. He and Francis stared at each other for a second, then Francis smiled and faded away. Dorran was still in the same position when Eli walked in. He looked at Eli. He had so many questions that he didn't know in what order to ask them.

Eli shuffled. "Maybe I shouldn't have used my key."

"What? No. I mean, why shouldn't you have? I gave it to you so you could use it."

Eli shrugged. "But we've been fighting."

And Dorran wasn't sure where they'd left things. He didn't know if they were still fighting, or if they were still together. He knew he should ask those questions, but it was late, and it was obvious Eli was exhausted. He was no doubt working overtime to solve Axel's murder. He needed rest, and Dorran was touched and glad that he'd come to him for it.

He got up and held a hand out. "Why don't we go to bed?"

"Are you sure? I should have called before coming."

"But you didn't. It doesn't change anything, though. You're always welcome here, even when we're fighting." Dorran hesitated. He didn't think it was the right moment to talk, but maybe Eli needed it. "Do you want to go to bed, or would you rather talk?"

Eli rubbed his face. His shoulders slumped, and Dorran could almost *feel* how tired he was. "Sleep, please. I know we need to talk, but—"

"We can do that tomorrow or another day. Come on." Dorran grabbed Eli's hand and pulled him toward the bedroom, turning off the light in the living room as he went.

They did need to talk, but most of all, Dorran had to think about what Francis had said.

Francis wasn't wrong. It might hurt Dorran to be kept a secret, but it was only to Eli's family, and hopefully, only until Eli felt they could take the news.

Dorran knew he didn't truly understand families and their relationships. His dad had died when he was a baby, and his mother was an alcoholic. He took care of her, but he didn't care what she thought. Why should he, when she didn't give a damn anyway? But Eli and his family were different. They were close, and Eli loved them and wanted them to accept him entirely, gay parts included. Dorran didn't doubt that one day, Eli would want to introduce a boyfriend to his parents.

He just hoped he would be that boyfriend.

Eli disappeared into the bathroom while Dorran settled in bed. He lay with his eyes open listening to the familiar sounds. He'd gotten used to having Eli around at night, and the past few days had been weird—and hard. Dorran hadn't realized how much Eli had wiggled his way into his life. They often ate dinner together, talking about their days, then spent the evening on the couch, Eli watching TV, Dorran reading. And of course, they shared a bed and woke up together.

Or they had until a few days ago.

Eli came out of the bathroom and turned the light off. He'd taken off his shirt and pants, but he'd kept his white t-shirt and boxer-briefs on. Dorran doubted anything but sleep would happen tonight, and he was okay with that. He wanted to have sex with Eli pretty much all the time, but this wasn't the right moment, for either of them. Eli needed to sleep, while Dorran was so lost in his feelings that he didn't know what he wanted. Being physical would make them feel close for a bit, but it wouldn't help long term.

They both had to think and decide what they wanted from each other and from their relationship.

Eli settled in the bed next to Dorran. They weren't touching, and Eli was tense, his front facing the ceiling. Dorran wasn't sure what to do. He wanted to roll toward Eli and snuggle against him, but was it the right thing to do? Was there a right thing to do at all in this situation?

Dorran didn't think he'd be able to sleep peacefully with Eli in his bed, not if they kept this distance between them. He rolled to the side and looked at Eli.

Eli would tell him if he didn't want him close. It would hurt, but at least he'd know.

Dorran shuffled until his front brushed against Eli's side. Eli looked down, and Dorran breathed easier when he saw he was smiling. "Can I?" he asked, holding his arm up and above Eli's waist.

"Of course. You don't have to ask, Dorran."

They both knew he did, but it didn't matter. Dorran plastered himself against Eli and sighed happily, closing his eyes and holding Eli close as Eli wrapped his arm around Dorran's shoulder.

Dorran had no idea what they were doing or what would happen to them as a couple, but right now, it didn't matter.

CHAPTER TWELVE

Waking up next to Eli was something Dorran would never get enough of. He hoped he wouldn't have to go without, and he hated how insecure he felt when it came to it. Eli still hadn't told him what he was going to do, though, and while Dorran was tempted to ignore his own feelings about the situation, he wasn't sure he could.

He'd been out to his family since he was sixteen. He'd never hidden the fact that he was gay. He didn't go shouting it on rooftops, and he supposed that since he didn't have a lot of people in his life, it didn't matter. He also realized that Eli's situation was very much different from his. He should probably be happy that Eli was out at work and not afraid to have his partner meet him, but it wasn't enough.

Dorran hated that it wasn't. He hated being a secret. He hated even more hearing Eli tell his mother that he wasn't dating anyone because it was a lie. Could he push Eli into coming out to his parents again, though? He understood why Eli didn't want to make waves. He'd been hurt when he'd told his family he was gay and his mother hadn't talked to him for months. Dorran didn't know how that felt, and he realized how lucky it made him. He'd never lost anyone because he was gay. His family, including his brother Chris, had accepted it, although it had taken Chris close to a decade. Charlie also hadn't cared one bit about it.

Eli, though, had come close to losing his mom, and he was probably terrified of it happening again. Was it right for Dorran to live in a situation he didn't want, though? To allow Eli to keep him on the sidelines when it came to his family? Or was Francis right? What would it change if Eli's family knew about Dorran?

Not much, probably. Dorran couldn't imagine they'd welcome him at Sunday lunch, at least not in the beginning. That was okay. He didn't want to push his presence on anyone. If he was honest with himself, what most bothered him was the way Eli's mother kept on trying to have him date women. He'd probably hate it even if she were pushing men at her son, but the women bit grated on his nerves. She was refusing to see the truth and to accept Eli the way he was. She'd be forced to if she knew about Dorran, though.

Not that this was the main reason Dorran wanted Eli to tell his parents about him. But this situation was much more complicated than he'd let himself admit in the beginning, and he hadn't been dealing with it the right way. He'd let his emotions and the feeling of being rejected take over instead of thinking about what this was doing to Eli, and that wasn't right.

God, he was an asshole.

"I wish you'd stop grimacing. It makes me feel like you're not happy about waking up with me," Eli said.

Dorran blinked. He'd been so focused on his thoughts that he hadn't realized Eli was awake. "I was just thinking." He settled on his side and smiled. "And trust me, there's nothing I like more than waking up next to you."

Eli's smile was hesitant, and Dorran hated himself for it. He wanted to be Eli's port in the storm, the person Eli could come to when he needed support and comfort. Instead, he'd made a fight out of every time they'd seen each other in the past few weeks.

Eli reached out and gently touched the bruise on Dorran's face. It was already fading, but it was still sore, and a reminder of what had happened to both of them. "I'm sorry I reacted the way I did."

Dorran frowned. "What do you mean?"

"I should have stayed with you the night you were attacked. It wasn't right for me to leave in a huff."

"I should have been nicer to you. You were worried. I know that. Yet I pushed until you were forced to leave. I'm glad we didn't start yelling. I don't think I could have stood it, not that day."

"Maybe, but I still feel like shit about it. You were probably scared and worried, and you lashed out. And *I* was scared and worried for you, and instead of dealing with that, I panicked and pushed you away."

Dorran grabbed Eli's wrist and squeezed. "How about we agree to forget about it? We were both tired, and the day hadn't been an easy one. You're under a lot of stress because of Emanuel's case. I shouldn't have pushed, and you shouldn't have left, but I think you did the right thing. I wasn't up for a fight then, and it would only have hurt both of us."

Eli nodded, but he was still serious. He stroked his fingertips along Dorran's cheek. "I want you to know that I meant it, though."

"What?"

"That we're a team. I never stopped loving you, Dorran. I didn't think I'd ever see you again, especially not after almost ten years, but I'm not going to let you go easily. I know that what we have isn't perfect, but I'm trying. I swear."

Dorran's chest felt painful. Eli never spoke about his feelings. He grunted and grumbled and told Dorran he loved him sometimes, but he never went in depth, and maybe that was one of the reasons Dorran was so freaked out about the fact that he was a secret. If Eli could hide him from his parents, did that mean he could easily dismiss him from the rest of his life, too?

Dorran knew that wasn't true, but hearing Eli tell him he loved him made him feel better. "I love you, too, and I'm not going anywhere."

"You're not happy."

Dorran wasn't sure how to answer that. "I'm not unhappy, either. I love you, and I love being with you. I won't deny that being kept a secret from your family hurts, but I've been thinking about it, and I realize how selfish it is of me to push the way I've been doing."

Eli sighed and rolled to his back. He pulled Dorran close, and Dorran snuggled against his side. "I never meant to make you feel like I was hiding you, Dorran."

"I know."

"But it's only from my family, and only for now. I know I'm already out to them and that things should be easier, but nothing is ever easy with the Hayes. You should remember that."

Dorran chuckled. "I do." He remembered the Hayes well.

"Mom, well, it's true she's never accepted that I was gay. I think she's hoping that one day, I'll find the right woman. The fact that I've never brought a boyfriend home probably doesn't help. Just give me some time, okay? I'll do my best not to hurt you, and I'll start preparing Mom to the fact that I'll soon be bringing a guy home."

"You could start by telling them you've met someone, maybe?" Dorran had no idea if this was the right approach. He should probably stay out of it, but he wanted this to happen, both for him and for Eli.

They deserved to be able to live openly, just like any heterosexual couple.

Families were never easy to deal with, though. Dorran might not have had problems when he'd told his family he was gay, but he had plenty of them for other reasons, the main one being his mother's alcoholism. It was something Dorran and Eli would need to navigate together. Dorran was used to it by now, but even though Eli knew about it, he'd no doubt have things to say about the way Dorran and his sister dealt with it.

That was okay. Dorran and Eli were a couple, a team. They needed to learn to deal with things together instead of on their own like they were used to, and that included families.

They loved each other, but they still had a way to go. Dorran was going to make sure they had time to learn these things. He wasn't giving up on Eli.

He never would.

Dorran knocked on Emanuel's door and waited. He could hear Emanuel move inside the apartment, but he wasn't surprised when he didn't come to the door right away. After what Emanuel had told Dorran about his father, Dorran didn't doubt that he was terrified. He would be. Hell, he *was*, because if the man in his apartment had been there on the orders of Emanuel's father, that meant the man could be back and that Dorran needed to be extremely careful when he opened his door.

Emanuel's door cracked open. Emanuel peeked from the crack, then opened the door wider. "Dorran. I didn't expect you."

"Sorry to bother you."

"You're not bothering me. Come in."

Dorran was only half surprised to see the packing boxes against the wall. They were still flat, but it was a sign of what Emanuel was going to do, and Dorran hated it. "Have you heard from your father?" he asked. He didn't sit down because he suspected Emanuel wouldn't want him around for long.

Emanuel pushed his long hair back. "No, but he's going to call."

"Why do you think he hasn't yet?" The man had given his orders through his lawyer, and that had been bad enough. Dorran wasn't sure if him calling Emanuel would be worse or not, though.

Emanuel sat onto the couch. "Because he's playing with me. He already knows I'm going to do whatever he wants me to do. I can't risk it."

"You won't go to jail. Remember that print on the knife? Eli told me that while they haven't been able to identify it yet, they know it doesn't belong to you. They know it wasn't you."

Emanuel's smile was sad. "That's good, but that's not the problem."

"What is, then?" Dorran couldn't force Emanuel to stand up to his father — he was starting to understand that not everyone could deal with their family as easily as he did, and for good reasons — but he wanted to help if he could.

"What if my father hurts someone else? I didn't love Axel, but it doesn't mean I'm not sorry he was killed, Dorran."

"Of course you are."

"I can't take the risk that my father will have someone else killed. I can't live the rest of my life waiting for him to do something and isolating myself so I can be sure he won't hurt anyone else because of me."

Dorran sat on the couch next to Emanuel. "You know none of this is your fault, don't you?"

Emanuel shrugged. "I didn't stab Axel to death, but I was the one who put him in my father's path. I can't deny that."

"It was your father who killed him, though." Maybe.

Emanuel smiled. "I know that, Dorran. Thank you for trying to help me. It doesn't change the fact that while I do know my father is entirely at fault, I can't afford for more people to get hurt, and that's what's going to happen if I stick around."

"But—"

"What happened to your face, Dorran? You never told

me."

Shit. "I was assaulted. It was nothing."

"Sure it wasn't. Let me guess—the man who hurt you told you to stay away from me."

Dorran sighed. There would be no hiding the truth from Emanuel, not when he already knew it. "Yeah, he did. And as you can see, I'm not going to do it."

Emanuel patted Dorran's knee. "Maybe you should. He's not going to stop, and I don't want you of all people to get hurt. I'd never forgive myself."

Dorran leaned back against the couch. "There *has* to be a way to get his claws out of you. What about what you know about him?"

"What do you mean?"

"Well, he's an asshole, and he doesn't balk even at killing people. I doubt this is a recent development."

Emanuel snorted. "He's been doing this kind of thing my whole life. Why do you think I left as soon as I was eighteen and changed my name?"

"Okay, so he's always done this. You probably know a lot of stuff, right? Or at the very least, you suspect it."

Emanuel's eyes widened. "No."

"No, you don't know anything?"

"No, as in no, I won't blackmail my father. This is crazy, Dorran. You're going to end up in Axel's place if you try to do something like that. Besides, there's no way I can give you any details. He's always been cautious, and not because I'm his son and he didn't want me to find out what he did. He's never cared about that. He doesn't trust anyone, not even me, so he made sure I never found out any kind of detail I could use the way you want to."

"But it's the only way."

"It's an impossible way. Please, Dorran. You're going to get yourself killed."

"I've been through this kind of thing before."

"But not with my father. He's going to eat you for breakfast."

Dorran was aware of that, but he couldn't think of another way to keep the man at bay and to make sure Emanuel was safe. Dorran had no doubt that if Emanuel went back to his father, they'd never see each other again. He didn't know if Emanuel's father would go as far as killing him, but it might happen, and Dorran didn't want to risk it. He was going to have to make sure everything was perfect, though. He needed to find out more about Jacob Crawford's business and the people he killed. He didn't know how he was going to do that, but he'd find a way.

He wouldn't let Emanuel disappear.

Dorran didn't have many friends, and he wasn't going to lose any of them. He wanted the opportunity to become friends with Emanuel, real friends.

"Please, Dorran. Promise me you won't go after my father."

Dorran shook his head. "I can't do that."

Emanuel looked sad. "I was afraid you'd say that."

CHAPTER THIRTEEN

Dorran had decided to get some dirt on Emanuel's father so the man would stay away, but he had no idea where to start. If even Emanuel didn't have any details about what his father was up to, how was Dorran supposed to find out anything?

"Who pissed in your cereal?" Francis asked, startling Dorran.

Dorran glared at him. "I should put a bell around your neck."

Francis pulled onto the collar of his shirt. "You could try, but I'm pretty sure it would just fall to the floor."

"Then you have to find a way to announce yourself. I don't know, start singing before arriving or something."

Francis grinned and sat next to Dorran on the couch. The couch didn't dip, and there was no movement of the air, no smell that didn't belong to Dorran. It was strange, but Dorran was starting to get used to it. "I don't know that you'd want me to sing. I was always horrible at it."

Dorran rolled his eyes. "Find something else, then, unless you want me to have a heart attack one of these days."

"Well, I can't say I would mind sharing this apartment with you."

"You already do."

Francis waved. "You know what I mean. I like you."

"I like you too, but I hope I won't become your permanent roommate for a while. No offense."

"None taken. And I hope we'll get to have a third, grumpy

102

roommate when it happens?"

Dorran groaned. "If you're talking about Eli, I don't know. We've made peace, but things still feel a bit fragile, and I'm not sure what to do about that."

Francis patted Dorran's knee, or at least he tried to, but Dorran couldn't feel anything. It didn't seem to matter to Francis, though, because he didn't even react. "Give it time. The important thing is that you and Elijah talked. Everything else will come in time."

"I'm going to tell him you call him Elijah."

"Please do. Maybe he'll finally admit I exist, then."

Dorran doubted it would be easy to make Eli accept ghosts existed. He hadn't yet, and he'd seen Francis and felt him more than once. "I'm working on that."

Francis wiggled his eyebrows. "That's what you call it these days?"

"Have you been spying on us?" Dorran asked, his cheeks feeling warm.

"I know you don't like it, so I try to stay in the spare bedroom when you disappear into yours."

Dorran supposed he should be thankful for that. "Thank you."

Francis gave him a pleased smile. "You're welcome. And give it time. You two love each other, that much is obvious. Relationships are hard work, but they're rewarding when you find the one man that is made for you."

"And you think *Eli* was made for me?" Dorran wasn't sure he believed that. Wouldn't he and Eli have stayed together if they were meant to be?

"Again, it's obvious to me. Was he the reason you looked like you wanted to stab the couch when I came in? What has he done this time?"

"Nothing. I told you we talked. No, this didn't have anything to do with him."

Francis rubbed his hands together. "Who did it have to do with, then?"

Dorran couldn't help but laugh. "You're such a gossip." He sighed, the humor fleeing him. "I was thinking about Emanuel, actually. He wants to obey his father's orders and go back home."

"Oh, no. His father is going to eat him alive."

That wasn't how Dorran would have put it, but Francis wasn't wrong. "Yeah. I've been trying to find a way around it, but he's convinced his father won't stop for anything, and honestly, I'm not sure he isn't right. His father sounds like a piece of work."

Francis pouted. "I wish I could become solid. Then I'd go find the man and take care of him. He wouldn't know what hit him, and no one would ever find proof it was me. Hell, no one would see me, since I'm invisible to most people."

Dorran frowned. "I know you can move around, but I thought you had to stay close to either the apartment or whatever you hitch a ride on." That was how he'd come with Dorran and Eli when Dorran's brother Chris had been arrested.

Francis grinned. "I've been testing this, and it's getting easier for me to move away from the apartment. I suppose there *are* perks to getting old."

Dorran rolled his eyes. "You're not getting old. You'll *never* get old."

"You know what I mean. Carole has been helpful, too."

Dorran blinked. "Carole?"

"I went home with her once. I love this place, but sometimes, I want to see more than these four walls. She taught me how to get home, and she told me that the more I do something, the easier for me it'll become, and that includes moving around."

"So it's possible? I didn't know that."

Francis shrugged. "I didn't, either. I guess most ghosts

stick to the place where they died or a place they were close to while alive. I'm not most ghosts, though, and nothing is going to stop me from taking a vacation to the Bahamas."

Dorran blinked. "The Bahamas?"

He suspected Francis' cheeks would have flushed if he'd still been alive. "Yes. It was on my bucket list. I'm not at the point where I can go that far yet, but I've been training."

"So hypothetically, you could leave this building and go to another one in town?"

Francis cocked his head. "I could, yes."

"Wherever in town?"

"What do you have in mind, Dorran?"

Dorran wasn't sure it could work, but what alternatives did he have? "I was talking to Emanuel, and I came up with a plan, sort of. He's not on board with it, though, and I'm not sure how to manage on my own."

"It's that *sort of* that scares me but go ahead."

"I want to blackmail Emanuel's father into leaving Emanuel alone."

Francis blinked. "Blackmail? You mean you want to threaten Jacob Crawford with exposing all his dirty little secrets unless he leaves his son alone?"

"Exactly."

"Well, at least I like you. I could have been stuck with someone I hated for eternity, and I have to say you're pretty, so I won't mind sharing my space with your ghost too much."

Dorran sighed. "I know it's dangerous, and I had no idea how to find the info I need until you said you could move around town now."

Francis' eyes widened. "You want *me* to blackmail the guy?"

"I wish you could, since you're already dead and everything, but no. I'll take care of that bit. What I want you to do, if you're okay with it, is find dirt on Crawford. You can sneak into his office and listen to his business. You can even find the bodies he buried, right?"

Francis grinned. "I knew there had to be a reason why I stuck around. This is going to be so much fun."

Dorran wasn't sure he'd have called it fun, but at least they had a plan, and a way to execute it. It was more than what he'd had even ten minutes ago. "So you'll do it?"

"Of course I will. Worry about nothing, my friend. I'll find the dirtiest dirt on Jacob Crawford, and I'll bring it back to you." He paused and frowned. "But how are you going to get proof of what he did?"

"I don't think I'll need it." Or at least, Dorran hoped he wouldn't. "Wouldn't you freak out if someone you didn't know told you about all the people you killed and where they're buried? I mean, I guess he could try to move the bodies, but depending on how many there are and where they are, it could be hard. No, I think that just making him aware I know will be enough. I'll tell him I won't say anything if he leaves Emanuel alone."

"What's your boyfriend going to think of that?"

Shit. "I don't know. I mean, like you said, it's not like I'll have proof, right?"

"What if I find proof?"

"Then I'll tell Eli." Because he'd never talk to Dorran again if he didn't. Besides, it would be a win-win in that case. Emanuel's father would go to jail, and Emanuel would be safe either way.

Francis grinned. "We have a plan, then."

"I guess we do."

With Francis now gone to spy on Crawford, Dorran decided to talk to Emanuel again. He knew Emanuel wouldn't like what he was doing, and he wasn't about to tell him about Francis, but he wanted his friend to know that he *was* doing something to help. They hadn't seen each other in a few days, and Emanuel had to be climbing the walls with worry.

Dorran hadn't expected to find him packing.

The apartment looked oddly empty without all the art supplies in the living room. It still smelled like they were there, though, and Dorran hung onto that. He wasn't sure when it had become imperative for him that Emanuel stay. He liked Emanuel, but they weren't friends, not close ones.

He'd like them to be, though. He needed more friends. He loved Charlie, but Charlie had Theresa, and they were taking the next step in their life by living together. Charlie didn't have as much time for Dorran as he did before, just like Dorran didn't have as much time for him since he and Eli had gotten back together. It was okay — it was part of growing up, and they'd always be friends — but Dorran liked Emanuel. Even if they never ended up being close, he hated the thought of anyone being forced into something by their parents of all people. Knowing the kind of man Jacob Crawford was made everything worse.

"You've made your decision," he said, crossing his arms over his chest.

Emanuel rubbed the back of his neck. He'd pulled his hair up into a bun, and for once, his clothes weren't splattered with paint. No, his t-shirt was depressingly clean. "I wasn't the one who made it."

"Your father did."

"Yes. And I know what you want to do. I can't, though. Dorran. I don't want you to get hurt. I've already lost Axel."

Even though Emanuel hadn't been in love with Axel, they'd still been together, and Emanuel had cared for him. Dorran had lost sight of that a few times, but he needed to remember that Emanuel was frightened and grieving. Going against the man behind it had to feel like an impossible feat to him.

Dorran wanted to tell him what was happening, but he wasn't sure how Emanuel would take it. Still, he looked like he needed hope, even if it was only a promise. "I'm looking into your father's past."

Emanuel's eyes widened. "I told you not to do that."

"I know. And I ignored you."

Emanuel huffed. He didn't look angry, which was something. He *did* look worried, though, and Dorran wasn't sure how to reassure him. He couldn't tell him that Francis would be doing all the hard and dangerous work, and that was probably the only thing that would make him feel better.

"You're going to get hurt," Emanuel said. He pulled his hair free and combed it with his fingers.

"It's a possibility." Especially once Dorran contacted Stone, the lawyer. He wasn't about to directly call Emanuel's father—even he wasn't that crazy—but he had no doubt that Stone would relay his message. Until then, though, he was safe thanks to Francis.

"Why are you doing this?"

"Because it's the right thing to do." Dorran stayed on the couch and mourned the loss of the colorful painting that had been hanging on the wall there. "You should have someone, someone you can trust and who will help you."

"And you decided to be that someone? I might already have other people to help me."

"Maybe." But Dorran doubted it. He'd been observing Emanuel since he moved into the building. It was true that Emanuel liked to go out, especially at night, but even when he brought home one-night stands or boyfriends, Dorran doubted he got close to them, not in a non-physical way. Emanuel was lonely, or at least Dorran suspected he was. He'd never seen him with a friend, not someone who'd come back to the apartment. His boyfriends didn't last long, although usually, they didn't get out of the relationship by dying. Emanuel also didn't have family, not family who cared anyway.

But he had Dorran, even though he might not want to have him.

"I promise I won't get hurt," Dorran said.

Emanuel snorted. "Of course you will if you play around with my father. But nothing I tell you will stop you, will it?"

"Not right now." Dorran was hell-bent on helping Emanuel, and he would.

Emanuel sighed and flopped onto the couch. Somehow, he managed to make even that movement graceful. "All right."

Dorran blinked. "All right?"

"Yeah. You're going to get yourself killed whether I like it or not. At least if I tell you the little I know, you'll be able to focus on stuff, and hopefully, it won't be as dangerous as you walking to my father's front door and telling him you know he killed people."

Dorran chuckled. "I wouldn't have done that."

"Sure you wouldn't have."

"I know he's a dangerous man, Emanuel. I'm not underestimating him, I promise. I can't tell you what I'm doing exactly, but I *can* promise you I'll get results. The most dangerous part will be when I have to contact him and tell him that if he doesn't leave you alone, I'm handing everything off to the press and possibly the police."

Emanuel grimaced. "You have a death wish."

"Nah. Eli will protect me." And he would, but since Dorran wasn't telling him what he was up to, he'd probably be too late if Dorran needed him.

He was going to be *pissed* when he found out what was happening. That wasn't going to make Dorran stop, though.

"Does he know about this?"

Dorran snorted. "God, no. He'd tie my ass to a chair if he knew what I was planning. But I'll have to tell him if I find proof of anything."

"You won't. My father has been at this for decades. He's perfected it. He knows what he's doing, and he doesn't leave proof around."

Maybe not for the police or anyone else with a pulse to find, but Dorran had a secret weapon. "We'll see. Is there anything at all you can tell me that would help me? Names, places, things like that. I'll take anything you can remember."

Emanuel sighed and leaned back against the couch. He rolled his head and peered at Dorran as if he were trying to read him. Maybe he was, but Dorran wasn't sure he was getting the answers he was looking for. "I told you I was never told anything."

"Maybe not, but you lived with him until a few years ago, right?"

"Yeah."

"I'm sure you noticed things. Even if you tried to stay as far away from him as you could, you shared a house."

"That house was huge. But yeah, you're right. I did notice stuff, and while I'm not a hundred percent sure of anything, I guess it should be enough to give you a place to start."

Dorran was finally getting somewhere. He leaned forward and tried to keep the eager expression off his face. "I promise you I'll be safe for now."

"You can't promise that, not when it comes to my father. But since my warnings aren't going to stop you, I might as well tell you." He licked his lips and closed his eyes. "Garrett Furlon. I'm pretty sure my dad killed him four years ago, or that he had him killed anyway."

Dorran rushed to get his phone out of his pocket so he could take notes. He didn't know if Emanuel would tell him anything useful, but what he was saying was more than what Dorran had right now.

CHAPTER FOURTEEN

Dorran was going crazy.

He glared at the TV even though he had no idea what movie he was watching. He'd turned it on because he needed a distraction, but it wasn't working.

It had been three days. Three days since he'd told Francis what Emanuel had said about his father. Three days since Francis had disappeared with the promise that he'd do everything he could to find proof of the stuff Emanuel's father was up to.

Three days since Dorran had seen him.

It wasn't even that he missed the ghost — although he did, because Eli hadn't come around much, either, and Emanuel was locked away in his apartment, still packing or hiding, Dorran wasn't sure. He hadn't gone back because he didn't want to push Emanuel, who clearly wanted to be left alone. Dorran wasn't offended, and he had other stuff to focus on, like his job, his boyfriend, and the fact that his spy ghost hadn't checked in yet.

Dorran couldn't help but be worried for Francis even though he knew he shouldn't. Francis would be fine. Not only was he already dead, but he was also invisible to most people unless he actively wanted them to see him. That was why sending him off to spy on Jacob Crawford had been a good idea. Dorran hated thinking about him being in the same room as Crawford, though, maybe having to witness something no one should see.

But Francis was doing something. Eli was doing

something, too, since he and Mel were still investigating Axel's death. And what was *Dorran* doing? He was staring at his TV.

Sometimes, he hated his life.

It wasn't that he wanted to be part of the investigation. He'd already been through enough with the last two he'd ended up involved in. He knew Eli was doing what he could to be sure Emanuel wasn't going to be dragged back to jail, and since Emanuel was packing and planning to move back with his father, Crawford would probably lay low for a bit.

Dorran tapped his fingertips on his knee. What more could he do? He was planning to use what Francis found out to make sure Crawford left Emanuel alone, but maybe he could do more.

The best way to make sure Emanuel didn't go back to jail would be to prove he didn't have anything to do with Axel's death. That would be possible if Dorran found out who the killer was. He was tempted to believe Emanuel when he said it had to be his father, but what if it wasn't? What if someone else had killed Axel?

Of course, there was the detail of the knife having been found under Emanuel's couch, but Dorran didn't think it would be hard for anyone to follow Axel to Emanuel's apartment to find out where it was, then later break in and place the knife. That was obviously how things had gone, so the question was, *who* had done it?

Had Emanuel's father hired someone, or had he taken advantage of what someone else had done? Eli hadn't told Dorran whether the print belonged to someone involved in the case, and Dorran knew better than to think he would. He and Mel would have arrested someone if they'd been able to, though, so Dorran doubted that print belonged to anyone he'd met.

But did Eli have the print of, say, Axel's ex-wife and her

father? Dorran had a hard time imagining Maggie Ford killing her ex and having the state of mind to take the knife to
Emanuel's apartment, but it wasn't like he knew her well.
Still, if he thought about her killing Axel, maybe in a moment
of anger, he could easily imagine what she might have done
once Axel was dead.

She'd have called her father.

The man had been protective of her, maybe even too much.
Dorran couldn't imagine his mother doing anything like that
for him, but he realized that the relationship he had with her
wasn't what most people thought of when they thought of
mother and son.

So maybe Maggie had killed Axel. Maybe she'd panicked
once she realized what she'd done. The print could be hers or
her father's, if he'd helped her get away with it. Wouldn't Eli
have their prints, though? Wasn't that how that worked? The
police took the prints of the people involved to be able to
strike them out as suspects — or to arrest them if they were
guilty. So they would know if Maggie or her father had anything to do with the murder, right? And they would have arrested either of them. And what about Axel? He'd told Dorran
he didn't know the man who'd killed him. He could have lied,
but why?

Maybe whoever the print belonged to had a reason to have
their print on the knife. The only one Dorran could think of
was if Maggie had been in Axel's apartment, maybe when
he'd moved in, or when she'd brought him their kids.

Dorran groaned. He really wasn't good at this, was he?
Emanuel was convinced his father was behind the murder,
and he was probably right. Could Dorran forget about Maggie and her father, though? They had a motive to kill Axel,
Maggie, especially. Her father had behaved like he'd do anything to protect her, so he'd probably step in if she called him
after she'd killed Axel. Dorran could imagine *him* taking the

knife to Emanuel's apartment and hiding it so Emanuel would be arrested.

Was that what had happened? Or was Emanuel right when he said his father had hired someone to kill his boyfriend and to make sure he was blamed for it so his father could swoop in, save him from jail, and demand he go home, or else?

Dorran had no idea, but since Francis was investigating Emanuel's father, maybe he should see what he could find out about Maggie and her father. She hadn't wanted to talk to him a second time, but maybe her father would. Dorran couldn't imagine it would be a pleasant conversation, but he had to do something. Talking to the man might give him clues as to what had happened.

There was a soft knock, then the sound of a key in the front door lock. Dorran checked the time, smiling when he saw it was still early enough that he and Eli could have dinner together. His smile widened when Eli stepped in, holding a pizza box. The smell of garlic and tomato sauce made Dorran's stomach rumble, and he put down the book he'd been trying to read along with trying to watch TV.

Neither had worked anyway.

"I wasn't expecting you," he said, getting up from the couch and taking the box from Eli's hands. He hesitated, then leaned forward and kissed the corner of Eli's mouth.

Eli's eyes widened, and he leaned closer, snaking his now free arm around Dorran's waist and pulling him closer. He kissed Dorran full on the mouth, and Dorran melted against him.

He didn't want to lose this. He didn't want to lose *Eli*. He thought they were managing pretty well, considering everything. Their relationship wasn't smooth sailing, but then, he hadn't expected it to be. Things were never easy with Eli, but that didn't mean Dorran wasn't up for the challenge.

He'd meet Eli's family again, eventually. He knew that. He

hated being a secret, but he'd hate losing Eli even more, especially after Eli had promised him that he was just trying to take things slow as to not freak out his parents.

Dorran believed him. He wasn't going to wait forever, but they hadn't been together that long, so he wanted to give Eli some leeway. Eli knew his family better than Dorran ever had, and he thought this was necessary.

It still hurt to hear him tell his mother that he wasn't dating anyone, but Dorran could deal with it. He'd have to remind himself of what he'd miss out on if he broke up with Eli.

Things were still slightly tense when they sat down to eat the pizza. Dorran was glad for not having to cook, but he couldn't deny it would have made things easier. He'd have had something to focus on, but as it was, he couldn't stop looking at Eli.

Eli wanted him in his life. He'd made that clear. And Dorran *wanted* to be in his life.

Did Eli's family really matter? It probably would eventually, but right now, maybe Dorran *was* making things bigger than they were. He didn't want to think about it anymore, though. He felt like he hadn't thought about much else recently. He wanted to focus on Eli and what they had, not on Eli's parents.

So he did.

He hooked his ankle around Eli's leg, smiling at him when Eli looked at him in surprise. Dorran didn't give him an explanation. He smiled back and took a bite of his pizza slice.

He didn't want to talk. They'd already talked about their situation too much, and Eli would go all tense if Dorran brought it up. "How's the investigation going?" he asked instead.

Eli paused, his pizza slice hallway to his mouth. "I shouldn't tell you anything about it."

"I know, and you don't have to if you think it's for the best.

You can just tell me if you think Emanuel is going to be dropped as your main suspect."

Eli sighed and put the pizza down. "I told you, I never actually thought he'd done it. I just don't have the proof of that."

"What about that print?" Dorran knew it was as easy and fast to identify a print as they showed on TV, but still.

"It's a mess. It's only partial, and it's smudged, almost like someone tried to clean it but didn't quite manage."

"Like someone would have if they'd decided to put the blame on Emanuel."

"Yeah."

"Do you think you're going to manage identification?"

"Probably? The technicians didn't make any promises, but they said it was possible. Of course, that'll only be the first step. It'll tell us who the killer is, probably, but we'll have to get more than that."

Dorran patted Eli's hand. "You will. You and Mel are good at this." He rubbed his legs against Eli. For once, he didn't want to talk about the case. It was important—life-changing for Emanuel—but Dorran wanted this evening to be about him and Eli, nothing else. "Are you done already?" He tilted his chin toward the pizza.

Eli arched a brown. "Well, I was going to eat more, but you look like you'd rather do something else."

Dorran laughed. "Race you to the bedroom." *This* was what he liked. Eli could be quite serious, but sometimes, he and Dorran played around, and it was *everything*.

Dorran's chair almost tipped over when he got up. He rushed toward the bedroom, thankful he didn't have a pet that might eat the pizza they were abandoning on the table. That might change one day, when and if he and Eli moved in together, but for now, it was convenient.

Dorran was the first to barrel into the bedroom. He already had his t-shirt halfway up his torso, and he stumbled against the dresser, narrowly avoiding slamming his hip against the corner. Luckily for him, the bed was right across the room, so when Eli grabbed his hips and pushed him, he fell right onto it. His legs were on the carpet, but he scrambled to get them onto the bed even as Eli grabbed the bottom of his jeans and pulled.

Dorran laughed. "That's not going to work if I don't open the button."

"What? You don't open it when you eat pizza? That's why you only eat a few slices."

Dorran laughed. He'd missed this, the carefree amusement, the fun they had when they weren't fighting. "And it explains how *you* can eat more than half a pizza. Your pants are already open, then?"

Eli used the hold he had on Dorran's ankle to flip him on his back. Dorran helped by opening his jeans and wiggling out of them as Eli pulled them off his legs. Eli dropped them on the floor and pressed Dorran's knees open. He crawled up the bed until he was face to face with Dorran. His eyes sparkled with what had to be amusement, and Dorran suspected he was looking at Eli in pretty much the same way.

Eli kissed him, but Dorran wanted to find out if he was right. He slid his hands down Eli's back, gave his ass a brief squeeze, then moved to Eli's front. Sure enough, his pants *were* open.

Dorran laughed. "I can't believe it."

Eli nipped at Dorran's jaw. "Shut up."

"Oh, I don't have anything against it. I think I like this quirk of yours. Gives easy access." Dorran slipped his hand into Eli's underwear and wrapped his fingers around his cock. It jerked against his palm. Dorran grinned. "Yep. I love it."

Eli rolled his eyes. "Wipe that smirk from your face and kiss me."

He didn't have to ask twice. Dorran loved kissing Eli. He surged up and smashed their lips together with a bit too much force, but it was easy to ignore the sting of pain. Eli's hands were on Dorran's torso, pushing up his t-shirt, stroking down his sides and teasing the elastic band of his boxer-briefs.

Dorran was done teasing. He wanted to be close to Eli, closer than he already was. He needed it after the past few weeks and the fights.

He pushed Eli's pants and underwear down Eli's hips, but with Eli stretched out between his legs, he couldn't get them as low as he wanted to.

"You're always so eager," Eli murmured.

"Who wouldn't be?"

Eli chuckled. "True. Stay right where you are, though."

Dorran wasn't sure he wanted to obey until Eli raised to his knees and started unbuttoning his shirt. Then Dorran couldn't look away.

Eli's body was gorgeous. His shoulders were broad, his skin pale, his chest and stomach covered with a light smattering of dark hair. The hair circled his nipples, framing them in a way that made Dorran want to suck them. His thighs were thick and hairier than his chest, but no less beautiful and sexy.

Eli threw his shirt to the side once he was done. He shuffled off the bed to take his pants—and, thank God, his underwear—off, too. Then he stood gloriously naked in front of Dorran. His uncut cock was hard, the head peeking from the foreskin. Dorran's mouth watered, but when he tried to sit up to suck Eli's cock, Eli stopped him.

"I told you to stay where you were."

"I wanna play," Dorran whined.

"And I want to take care of you. After everything I said and the way I've been treating you . . ."

Dorran's heart felt like it swelled with the love he felt for the man in front of him. "I don't want us to think about that right now."

"All right, but I still want to take care of you."

Dorran flopped his arms and his legs wide. "I'm all yours."

Eli looked him up and down. Dorran wasn't naked yet, but his t-shirt was bunched under his armpits, and his cock was pushing against the cotton of his boxer-briefs. "You are, aren't you?" Eli murmured.

Dorran's cheeks flushed, but he didn't deny it. He *was* Eli's, no matter how much they fought and the doubts that plagued him. Even if they did break up, he'd still be Eli's.

Dorran decided he needed to get naked to distract himself. He got rid of his t-shirt, then his boxer-briefs. He threw those at Eli's head, and instead of ducking, Eli grabbed them and raised them to his nose, making Dorran blush even harder. He didn't tell Eli how flustered the sight made him, but then, he didn't have to. Eli hadn't yet looked away from him.

He did now. He opened the nightstand drawer and took the lube out. They'd stopped using condoms a few months into their relationship. Dorran wouldn't have with any other man, but he trusted Eli with his life, and they knew each other well enough that he was sure Eli wouldn't cheat on him — and if he did, he wouldn't expose Dorran to any STD he might catch. But Eli had honor, and he wouldn't put Dorran's well-being in jeopardy.

Dorran stayed on his back, fully exposed. The position, the vulnerability of it, still made his stomach churn a bit, but he didn't move. It was easy to push those feelings away when Eli took his place between Dorran's legs again and opened the lube.

There was nothing to be afraid of. Eli wouldn't take advantage of Dorran's fragility.

He never did.

Eli was carefully slow as he prepped Dorran, to the point that Dorran wanted to yell at him to get a move on. He knew that would only get him the opposite of what he wanted, though. When Eli wanted to go slow, they went slow, and if Dorran protested, Eli went even slower. He could spend hours teasing and playing with Dorran's body, reducing him to tears and whimpers, and while that didn't sound like a bad idea, Dorran wanted Eli in him soon. He wanted to be that close to him again, to feel like the space between them wasn't there anymore.

Eli left Dorran gasping and opening his legs even more an attempt to get Eli closer. Dorran could tell there were at least three fingers inside him—the fullness, the stretch, were deliciously reminiscent of what he'd feel like when Eli's cock was finally inside him.

"I could make you come like this, couldn't I?" Eli asked. He was still hard, and Dorran wondered how he could be so calm. He wanted to climb the walls or throw Eli on his back and climb *him*.

"Is that really what you want, though?" Dorran asked, breathless. It was hard to think right now, and he was proud of himself for putting an entire sentence together.

Eli's lips curled into a wicked smile. "No, it's not."

He finally—*finally*—slipped his fingers out of Dorran. Dorran flexed his legs, hooking one of them behind Eli's back and trying to pull him closer. Eli moved at his own pace, though, grabbing the base of his cock and leaning forward, his gaze locked on Dorran's ass.

Dorran held his breath when Eli's cock breached him. He closed his eyes and focused on the sensation. They *were* one right now, connected at a level Dorran never wanted to lose. It wasn't merely physical, but that part helped him focus on Eli and on what they shared.

They were in love. That had to mean something. It had to.

"Breathe," Eli murmured as he pushed himself deeper into Dorran. He leaned forward and kissed Dorran's eyelids, his forehead, his lips. He was gentle and sweet, and everything Dorran could have wished for. He *was* enough.

Dorran hooked his arms around Eli's neck and wrapped himself around him. It made it hard for Eli to add force to his thrust, but the pressure and friction on Dorran's cock where it was trapped between them were enough to push Dorran toward orgasm. He held on, taking everything Eli had to give him — the tenderness and sweetness, the slow lovemaking he'd only known with this man.

"I love you," Eli gasped. Dorran could tell he was almost there, too, and he tightened his hold on him. He squeezed Eli's cock with his ass, grinning when Eli moaned.

They knew how to play each other's bodies by now, what to do and not to do — and how to make sure the other barreled to orgasm. Dorran continued massaging Eli's cock and leaned closer, pressing his face against Eli's neck and pressing light kisses to his skin. Once Eli started thrusting faster — a sure sign he was about to come — Dorran bit down.

Eli shouted. His dick twitched in Dorran's ass, but Dorran focused on his own cock now, on the friction that came from Eli's slowing movements and how Eli's hair felt. It prickled so nicely, especially when Dorran pushed his hips up for more pressure. He rutted against Eli until he came, spending between them, out of breath and sweaty.

Then he flopped on the bed, releasing Eli, who rolled to the side and pulled him close.

"We should clean up," Dorran said, but he had no intention on getting up.

Eli kissed his shoulder. "We will, later. Maybe after round two?"

Dorran snorted, but he knew it would probably happen. Eli was as eager as he was to be close, and what was closer than being in bed together, naked and still panting from their lovemaking?

CHAPTER FIFTEEN

Dorran knew that going to meet Axel's father-in-was was a bad idea. It would no doubt get him in trouble with Eli, and they were trying to make things work. He had to do it, though. He couldn't sit on his ass in his office waiting for Emanuel to be arrested again or for him to move back with his father.

So there he was, peering at Maggie Ford's house from his car. He'd seen her leave earlier with her two children, so he knew she wasn't home, but there was a truck parked in the driveway, and he hoped it was her father's. He had no idea where the man lived, and he wasn't about to ask Eli. He might be able to find out through social media, but it would be a stretch.

Dorran grinned when the sound of a motor running coincided with the appearance of the man he was looking for. Mr. Warren came around the corner of the house, pushing a lawnmower. He was heading for the front yard, which would be the perfect place for Dorran to talk to him.

Dorran got out of his car. Maggie's father didn't notice him until he was almost next to him, and for a second, Dorran wondered if he was going to try to run him over with the mower. He wouldn't put it past the guy, not with the way he was glaring.

Dorran raised a hand in a small wave. "Hello. Can I talk to you for a moment?" He could tell the answer would probably be no, but he didn't move from his spot on the sidewalk. He technically wasn't on the Ford property, and he wasn't going to risk it.

Mr. Warren turned the lawnmower off. "What do you want?"

"To talk to you."

"About Axel."

"Yes."

"My daughter told me you're not a cop."

"She's right. I'm not."

"Why are you asking questions, then? It's none of your business."

He was right — it wasn't. "It's just a few questions."

"That you don't need to ask. You should leave."

"I'm trying to find out what happened to your son-in-law."

"I already told you I don't care what happened to him. I'm *glad* he's dead for what he did to my daughter. I'll shake the killer's hand if the cops ever find out who did it."

Dorran had expected this, but he'd hoped to manage to get a few questions in before the rant started. "I just wanted to ask where you were on the night Axel was killed. The police found a print on the knife that was used to kill Axel, and they're going to identify the killer soon. I'm surprised they haven't yet." Eli had told Dorran the print was only partial and that it was deformed somewhat, so it made sense that he and Mel hadn't yet been able to tell who it belonged to. Warren didn't have to know that, though. Maybe being aware of the print would push him to confess or something.

Dorran could always dream.

That was the wrong thing to ask. Mr. Warren took a step toward Dorran, and while Dorran wanted to look confident, he was also scared shitless. Mr. Warren might have a beer gut, but that didn't mean he couldn't beat Dorran up for saying the wrong thing.

"What did you say?" Mr. Warren growled.

"I'm trying to help a friend, Mr. Warren. Please."

"By implying *I* killed Axel? God knows I might have if I'd had the chance, but I didn't need to because someone did it for me. Now get the fuck out of here, asshole. I don't want to ever see you again around this house, or around my daughter."

Dorran scurried back to his car before Warren could change his mind and decide he was in the mood to nail Dorran's ass to the wall after all. He slid into the driver seat and leaned back his head.

Okay, so that hadn't gone the way he wished it had. He hadn't expected Warren to confess to killing his son-in-law, but he'd hoped to get at least a few answers, especially about where Warren and his daughter had been the night Axel had been killed.

So far, Dorran had two theories about the murder — either Emanuel was right, and his father had hired a professional killer to kill Axel and put the blame on his son, or Warren or his daughter had killed Axel and had decided to try to get Emanuel to pay for it. Either way, Emanuel was screwed.

Dorran had no doubt that if the killer wasn't found, Emanuel would go back to jail. Without his father's lawyer, he probably wouldn't get out of it again, either. The only reason he *was* out was thanks to the print on the knife, and Dorran had no idea what was going on with that. He could probably find out, but would Eli tell him anything? Their relationship was getting better, and Dorran didn't want to rock the boat. Was what he had with Eli strong enough to make it through that kind of request, or would Dorran have to choose between them and keeping Emanuel out of jail?

Dorran already knew what he'd do if things came to that. He hated it, but he wouldn't be able to live with himself if Emanuel was arrested again, not when he knew his friend hadn't done anything.

Dorran was glad when his phone rang, and even happier

when he saw it was Charlie. He could do with a distraction. He doubted he'd manage to focus on work today anyway. "Hey."

"You sound weird. What happened?"

Dorran closed his eyes. "How do you do that?"

"Do what?"

"How do you know something happened?"

"It's a skill I learned over the years. Come on, tell me."

"Are you busy for lunch?"

"I can take an hour or so, as long as you come here."

"That shouldn't be a problem." It wasn't like Dorran had to go back to the office, although he probably should at least try to get a bit further ahead on the translation he was working on. He wouldn't get paid if he didn't hand it over, and he needed that money.

"Great. Meet me at that fast-food joint on the corner in half an hour."

Dorran grimaced. He wasn't looking forward to fast-food, but maybe he could order a salad or something. "Okay."

"And don't wrinkle your nose at the burgers."

"Fuck you, Charlie. You don't know me as well as you think you do:"

"You'll find that's wrong, but who am I to ruin your dreams."

Dorran was smiling when he hung up. Charlie always managed to do that—Dorran was more relaxed now, and while his problems were still very much there, he hoped he'd be able to ignore them for a little while. He needed to, because he'd go crazy otherwise.

So he'd go to lunch, he'd answer Charlie's questions about Eli and hope Charlie wouldn't find out that Dorran had decided to investigate Axel's case. Then he'd go home and hope Francis had finally found something, preferably some kind of solid proof that Emanuel hadn't had anything to do with his boyfriend's death.

Dorran was finally relaxed, so of course, that was when Charlie asked, "What's up, then?"

Dorran had managed to keep the conversation away from himself until now, but he was starting to suspect that Charlie had been humoring him. He didn't look like he was going to continue doing so. His gaze was fixed on Dorran, and when Dorran opened his mouth to give him a bullshit excuse, he arched a brow and meaningfully cocked his head.

Dorran sighed. "Where do you want me to start?"

"Oh, I'm not sure I like the sound of that. You have so much stuff going on that there's a place to start and go down from there? What happened to the old Dorran that barely left his bedroom and would talk my ear off about buying the wrong brand of cereal?"

Dorran's cheeks flushed. He wasn't that boring. Was he? "You're an ass."

"Mmm, but Theresa loves my ass."

Dorran grimaced. "Not something I want to think about. And I'm fine."

"Right. What's happening with Eli, then? The last time we talked, you weren't sure the two of you had a future, and since you didn't call me in tears, I suspect you're still together."

Dorran didn't particularly want to talk about that, but it was better than telling Charlie that he was using his ghost best friend to spy on one of the most ruthless men in town. "We are. We talked."

"And? Wait, let me guess. He promised you he needs time and that eventually, he'll tell his parents about you."

Dorran glared. "He did, and I believe him."

Charlie raised his hands. "I never said you couldn't. I like Eli, remember, and even though my family is okay, I know it can be hard to deal with them in some situations."

"Don't I know it."

Charlie smiled. "I know you do, but I also know that your situation is very different from Eli's. I'm happy you decided to give him a chance if that makes you happy, but I'm curious about it. You sounded so unsure the last time we talked."

Dorran leaned back in his chair. He pushed a piece of lettuce around in the bowl, wrinkling his nose. "I love him."

Charlie rolled his eyes. "Obviously. And he loves you."

"I know he does. And that's enough for now. Like you said, I also know how hard it can be to deal with family. Not in the same way, but maybe that's why I don't fully understand what Eli is going through. I don't care what my mother thinks about the choices I make. I couldn't care less if she decided to stop talking to me." Dorran loved her, or rather, he loved the memory of her, of the way she'd been when he was a child. Things were different now, and while he wasn't going to abandon her, he'd learned to shield himself and his heart from her.

She was an alcoholic, and she had no intention of changing that. Dorran had come to terms with it a long time ago, and he'd taught himself not to care.

Eli cared, though. He loved his parents and his brothers. He cared what they thought about him, and he wanted to make sure things went smoothly with them, or as smoothly as possible.

"So you're ignoring the being a secret part."

"For now. I know Eli isn't doing it because he's ashamed. He's trying to keep the peace with his family, and that's okay. I know he's not ignoring me or waiting for the best time to break up with me."

"He's going to tell them eventually."

"He is." Dorran had to believe that. "But he knows best how to deal with them. I haven't seen them since I was a teenager. So I'm going to give him time to smooth things over with them and ease them into realizing that he wasn't kidding when he told them he was gay." That had been the hardest part. They *knew* Eli was gay, even though they liked to ignore that part of him. They wouldn't be able to do it once Eli brought Dorran home, and Dorran was willing to give him the time he needed, no matter how uncomfortable it made him.

Charlie grinned. "Good boy."

"I'm not a dog."

"No, but I expected you to make your relationship explode. I'm proud of you for realizing that Eli *isn't* trying to hide you and that he really just needs more time. Family is hard, man. The important thing is that you and Eli will present a united front when the time comes."

Dorran didn't mind the heart to heart with his best friend, but he was glad when Charlie moved on to talking about his probable wedding. He hadn't asked Theresa to marry him yet, but Dorran suspected it was only a matter of time before he did. They were made for each other, and they were in love. They were ready to start this new chapter of their lives, just like Dorran was with Eli—although they weren't anywhere near ready to think about marriage. The thought didn't terrify Dorran like it might have once, though. He wasn't sure why, but he didn't mind.

"I have to get back," Charlie said. He didn't sound happy.

"We can meet again this weekend if you want?"

Charlie's expression lit up. "Maybe we can have a double date."

Dorran groaned, but he didn't mind. "I'll see what Eli thinks of it, but you know how his job is."

"He'll get a pass if he can't come or if he has to go, don't worry."

They headed toward the door. They'd been at the back of

the restaurant, so they had to cross the length of it to leave. Dorran frowned when Charlie froze. He turned to face his friend, but Charlie wasn't looking at him, he was staring at something that was now behind Dorran, and when Dorran started to turn to check, he grabbed Dorran's arm. "Don't."

"What's wrong?"

"Dorran . . ." Charlie sighed. "Give him time to explain himself, okay? Don't leave in a huff. You don't know what's happening."

"I don't know because you won't let me look."

Charlie let go, and Dorran turned. It took him a moment to find what Charlie was talking about, and when he did, he wished he hadn't.

Eli was sitting at a table, his back to the wall. A woman was next to him, smiling and agitating her hands as she talked. While Dorran watched, she reached out and touched Eli's arm, leaving her hand there. She leaned closer, pushing her hair back with her free hand.

And Eli didn't say anything.

He didn't move toward her like she was doing with him, but he also didn't ask her to take her hand off his arm. He was listening to her, a small smile on his lips.

Dorran didn't know what to do. His first instinct was to assume something was up, but he forced himself to calm down and to look at things as objectively as he could.

Eli was gay, so there was no way he was cheating on Dorran with that woman. She did seem affectionate with him, though, and Dorran didn't know who she was. Eli didn't usually hide things from him, not since the debacle with his cat.

So what was going on?

"What are you going to do?" Charlie asked.

"I don't know." Dorran knew it would be weird if he left without stopping by Eli, and he didn't want to. Eli needed to realize Dorran had seen him.

Dorran moved forward. He heard Charlie suck in a breath, but he didn't stop. Instead, he plastered a fake smile on his lips. "Eli. I didn't know you'd be having lunch here," he said as he got to the table.

He knew Eli hadn't wanted him to know he was by the way he paled. His expression went blank. "What are you doing here?" he asked.

"I had lunch with Charlie. He works close by."

The woman Eli was with was looking alternately at him and Dorran. She didn't introduce herself, something for which Dorran was glad.

Eli cleared his throat. "This is Gemma."

Dorran nodded at her. She smiled, although not as widely as she had with Eli. "Nice to meet you," she said.

Dorran's stomach churned. "Same." He was ready to bet that Eli's mother had something to do with it. She'd been pushing him to date women, and it looked like she might have managed to convince him. Maybe Eli was just trying to keep her happy. Dorran knew he wouldn't do anything with Gemma, but it still hurt.

The fact that he hadn't *told* Dorran about this hurt. The fact that Dorran didn't know for sure why Eli had decided to have lunch with Gemma hurt. Dorran hated it, and he didn't want to be bothered by it, but he couldn't change what he felt. He wouldn't have been happy if Eli had told him about this, but he might have understood.

"I'm going home," he said. "I'll see you when I see you."

"Dorran—"

Dorran shook his head. "It's fine, Eli. Really. Don't worry about me. Have a nice lunch."

Dorran didn't run out of the restaurant, but it was a close thing.

Chapter Sixteen

Dorran was moping. He'd been ignoring Eli's phone calls—he knew Eli wanted to explain what had happened, and he'd listen to that explanation as soon as he felt he could. Right now, he needed some time to deal with what he felt.

He knew he was being ridiculous. Eli hadn't been doing anything wrong, even though it had looked like he was on a date. Dorran knew he hadn't been—he was gay, for fuck's sake, no matter what his mother might hope for—but it was one more indication that maybe Dorran had been right after all.

Was Eli *ever* going to tell his mother about him? Or was he going to continue to let her introduce him to women and push him into dating them, even though it was fake-dating?

Or maybe Dorran should give him more time.

He groaned and hit the back of his head against the couch. He didn't know what to do. He wanted to be with Eli, but this situation was hurting him. He'd talk to Eli before making any decision, of course, but he hated this.

"What happened now?"

Dorran startled at the sound of Francis' voice. He glared at him. "A bell, Francis."

Francis rolled his eyes and settled next to Dorran on the couch in what seemed to now be their usual position. "You keep threatening to do that, but we both know you won't."

"Only because the bell wouldn't stay on you. You're not solid."

Francis pouted. "You hurt me."

"What, I shouldn't remind you you're dead."

"I know I am, and it's okay. I've gotten used of it."

Dorran's phone vibrated on the coffee table, but he didn't bother looking at it. He knew it was Eli, even though he'd texted him to tell him to give him some time.

"You're not going to answer that?" Francis asked, eying the phone.

"You're not going to tell me why you're here?"

"Touché. But you know I'm here because I live here, right?"

Dorran rolled his head to the side so he could look at Francis. "What did you find out?" He hoped Francis *had* found something. He needed things to go well at least in some parts of his life.

"I've been hanging around Emanuel's father. Emanuel was right—the man is a piece of work. My skin hasn't stopped crawling."

"Technically, your skin *can't* crawl."

Francis narrowed his eyes. "You know what I mean."

Dorran smiled. "All right, I'll be serious. What did you find out?"

"Apart from the fact that Crawford seems to have a hand in everything bad in this town?"

"We already knew that, though."

"I've listened to him threatening people, setting up deals for everything, from drugs to prostitutes."

"Do we have some kind of proof of that? I mean, I'm pretty sure the police already know about this, to be honest. They don't have proof, though, which is the problem."

"Nothing you can use. I might have something else, though." Francis leaned forward. He reached for a pen Dorran had left on the coffee table, but he stopped before touching it. He sighed and dropped his hand. "Crawford talked about someone he killed."

That got Dorran's full attention. "What?"

"I know where the man is buried, how he was killed, and by whom."

"By Crawford."

"Yes. And from what Crawford said, he wasn't as careful as he should have been when it comes to leaving clues. He doesn't seem to be, not in this kind of occasion."

"This kind of occasion?"

"That man isn't the only one Crawford has killed, Dorran. I know of a lot of bodies he had buried or partially destroyed. I can tell you where they are. I managed to check in on a few, and they're there."

"Are there enough of them that Crawford won't be able to move them all once I tell him I know about this?"

"I'll be going back, of course, but I think so. I can't say I'm enjoying this, but I want to help Emanuel. Besides, it's a good way to train my ability to move around and stay away from the apartment for a longer length of time. Carole says it'll become easier the longer I do it, and this seems like the perfect reason to do it."

"How did you manage to find out about this?" Dorran couldn't imagine Crawford routinely spoke about the people he'd killed.

"I didn't just spy on him. I followed several people I saw him talk to, and I sat in on enough meetings to be bored to death—if I wasn't already dead, of course."

"Thank you, Francis."

Francis waved. "Please. I'm doing this for Emanuel, not for you."

"I'm feeling the love."

"You know what I mean. You'll be fine, even though you and your boyfriend are both stubborn asses. But Emanuel is alone, and he needs help."

"He's not alone. He's my friend."

Francis' smile was soft. "I know. You're the best thing that happened to this apartment, Dorran."

"It's just an apartment." But Dorran's life had changed when he'd moved in. He'd been shot at, assaulted, had started seeing ghosts, had gotten back with Eli, had made friends with Emanuel. He didn't want to go back to what he'd had before.

"You can keep telling yourself that. Where are you going?"

Dorran had gotten to his feet. He stretched, hoping the kink in his back would be gone by the time he needed to sit down at his desk to work. "I'm going to talk to Emanuel, see if he can tell us where his father was when some of the people you found out about died."

"Then maybe you should write down who they were and when they died before going."

"I know that." The truth was that Dorran wanted out of his apartment for a bit. Eli wasn't done calling even though Dorran had texted him that they were okay, and Dorran knew he wouldn't stop until he got an answer. They might both be stubborn, but Eli especially so, to the point that Dorran had felt the need to give up a few times even though he'd known he was right and Eli wrong. It probably wasn't the healthiest way to deal with things, but it was either that or fight, and Dorran hated to fight, especially with Eli—especially about stuff that didn't matter.

"You're going to have to talk to him sooner or later," Francis pointed out after he'd given Dorran a list of names and Dorran's phone had rung twice.

"I will, just not now."

"Don't wait too long, Dorran. I don't know what happened this time, but you know things will only get worse if you wait."

Dorran was aware of that, but he didn't confirm it. Francis

was already smug enough as it was.

Dorran left him behind in the apartment — Emanuel didn't know about Francis or ghosts in general, and Dorran didn't think it was the right moment for him to find out. He knocked on Emanuel's door, half expecting him to be gone. Dorran checked in on him every day, and every day, he wondered if he'd find him home or if he'd be back at his father's house.

The door opened. Emanuel looked tired, his hair hanging limply around his face. It was dirty, something that surprised Dorran because of the pride Emanuel had in his hair. He didn't ask what was wrong, though. He already knew the answer to that question. "Can we talk?"

Emanuel stepped aside. The apartment looked like he'd stopped packing when Dorran had told him he was going to try to blackmail his father. It gave Dorran hope that Emanuel trusted him to be able to do this. It was more trust than he had in himself.

"I found some stuff about your father," he said.

Emanuel sighed. "What?"

"Do you think you could go over this list of names and dates and tell me if you recognize anything? And that you can tell me where your father was on those days, if he has an alibi, that kind of thing."

"An alibi? That means all these people are dead, doesn't it?"

Dorran hadn't been planning on keeping it a secret, so he nodded. "Yeah. I think your father killed them. I know it's hard to believe, but—"

"It's not. I told you, I know my father. He might have managed to keep me out of his business once I told him I didn't want anything to do with it, but that doesn't mean I'm hiding my head in the sand when it comes to him. I know who he is. I know *what* he is. That's one of the reasons I left."

"Do you want to help me, then? I'll keep your name out of

it when I contact his lawyer, but you can say no."

Emanuel's eyes blazed. It was the most emotion Dorran had seen in him lately, and he was glad for it. "I'll help. He killed these people. Even if you can't prove it, I want him to know that someone knows about it."

"I'll hand everything over to the police once this is over, though."

"I didn't expect anything different from you, Dorran."

Eli was waiting for Dorran when Dorran got back home.

Dorran wasn't surprised. He'd expected Eli to come around ever since he'd left the restaurant after having lunch with Charlie and stumbling on Eli having lunch with *Gemma*.

"Hey," he said, closing the door. He hoped Francis was either out or in his bedroom because he'd rather do this without an audience.

Eli was on the couch, but he got up. "You didn't answer my phone calls."

"I texted you why I wasn't answering."

"You said you needed time, but I want to explain."

Dorran was suddenly exhausted. "There's nothing to explain." There was plenty, actually, but Dorran wanted to go to bed and to stay there until tomorrow morning.

Eli grimaced. "Yeah, there's plenty to explain. I didn't know I was meeting Gemma today."

"So what, you stumbled onto her and decided to have lunch?"

"No. I was supposed to meet my mom."

Dorran blinked. "I don't get it."

Eli sighed and sat back down. He held out his hand, and while Dorran hesitated to take it, he did. He didn't want what was between them to end, and he couldn't help the hope at Eli's explanation. It wouldn't solve all their problems, but Dorran wasn't going to kick Eli out, no matter what he said.

Dorran sat next to Eli. Eli didn't let go of his hand, but he wrapped his other arm around Dorran's shoulders and kissed his temple. "Gemma and I are childhood friends in a way. We grew up on the same street, and we were friends as kids. We grew apart over the years, especially after we started high school. I hadn't seen her again until today, not since we graduated. She went off to college in another city."

"Okay." Dorran wasn't sure where Eli was going with this, but he was willing to wait it out.

"Anyway, my mom called a few days ago. She asked me if we could have lunch today. I didn't tell you because I know that talking about my parents, but especially my mother, hurts you."

Dorran had nothing to say to that. Well, almost nothing. "You could have told me. I know they're your family, no matter how much I hate the way they're treating you."

"I get that now."

"How did you end up with Gemma, then?"

"I didn't even know she was back in town. I got to the restaurant, and there she was. I thought it was a coincidence, but she said my mother told her I wanted to meet her."

"So she set up a blind date for you?" That sounded like Eli's mother all right.

"Kind of. Gemma knew she was meeting me, but I didn't."

"And when you realized that, you decided to have lunch with her."

"Yeah. I was already there, and it gave us a chance to catch up. She didn't know I was gay, so I told her, and when you left, and she asked about you, I told her you were my boyfriend."

"Is she going to tell your mom about it?"

"She said she wouldn't, and I believe her. We were never in love, Dorran. We were friends, and yeah, our mothers liked to tease us about getting married one day, but it was never like that. It was wishful thinking for my mother, and that's *all* it was, I swear. I would have told you about Gemma tonight."

Dorran settled closer to Eli and inhaled his familiar scent. "I'm not angry."

"I know. It's kind of obvious when you are."

Dorran chuckled. "I'm not angry, but I can't say I wasn't hurt when I saw you. I guess I shouldn't have jumped to conclusions, and I regret doing it. But knowing your mother keeps introducing women to you is making me paranoid, even though I know you'd never cheat on me."

"You're right, I wouldn't. I love you, and only you."

But sometimes, love wasn't enough. Dorran wanted it to be in this situation, though. He *needed* it to be. "So you and Gemma are friends."

"Yes, and *only* friends."

"Okay. You know your mother is going to continue introducing women to you, right? That's not going to change until she finds the right one for you, and since we both know there *is* no right woman for you out there . . ."

"I know. I'll talk to her and tell her to back off. She already called me a few times, no doubt to find out how the thing with Gemma went. I'll tell her we're only friends and that we won't ever be more."

Dorran trusted that Eli would and that he'd tell his mom to back off. He knew enough about her to know she wouldn't, though. She wanted Eli to be happy, and for her, that meant having him married and possibly popping out a few kids to make her a grandma again. Dorran hadn't seen her in a long time, but he doubted she understood that some people needed something else to be happy—*someone* else.

"I'm not going anywhere," he said, tilting his head up to look at Eli.

Eli cupped his cheek. "Are you sure? I know how hard this is for you."

"Do you? I mean, it's not like my mother is introducing me to ladies she thinks I'll want to have kids with."

Eli smiled. "No, but I can too easily put myself in your shoes. The thought of having to watch you take those ladies out for lunch makes me want to break something."

"I won't say *I* don't want to break something, but I understand, Eli. You love your mom, and she loves you. She's trying to do what she thinks is right, and you don't have the heart to tell her that she's wrong. You're also terrified of losing her because when you told her you were gay, she didn't talk to you for months. How am I doing so far?"

"You know me better than anyone else, and that includes my mother." Eli sighed. "Yeah, I'm afraid of all of that. She's never been an easy woman, and she's gotten it in her head that she needs to marry me off. And you're right. She does think that the right woman will *cure* me from being gay. Because she knows I am, no matter how hard she's trying to ignore it."

"You can't live that way forever." Dorran didn't even mean that Eli couldn't hide him forever. Even if they broke up, Eli would have to go through this, and Dorran couldn't imagine things were easy from his side, either.

"I know, and I'm not planning to." He took a deep breath, and Dorran felt his chest move up and down. "I'm going to tell her on Sunday."

Dorran pushed away. "On Sunday? You mean when you go for Sunday lunch?"

"Yeah."

"No, Eli."

Eli's eyes widened. "What? But I thought—"

"I do want you to tell her that we're together. I'm never *not* going to want that. But you can't tell her when you go home for Sunday lunch. That's the one day in the week where she has all her family with her. She's looking forward to it. She's

139

happy when you're all there. You can't tell her then."

Eli rubbed the back of his head. "When, then?"

"Take her out to lunch. Pick a quiet place, maybe somewhere familiar to her, somewhere quiet. Don't just blurt everything out, either. Remind her that you're gay, and *then* tell her about me if you think you should."

Eli shook his head. "I can't believe you want me to go easy on her. You've been miserable because of the way she's behaving."

"Yeah, but she doesn't know about me, does she? I doubt she'd try to get you to date anyone if she did."

"So you're saying it's my fault, not hers."

Dorran smiled and kissed Eli's cheek. "In part. She shouldn't force you into something she knows damn well you don't want, and you should have told her. I understand why you didn't, and I'm sure she will, too, once you give her time to wrap her mind around it. Don't push her too hard, but if you don't at least try, you'll never know if she can accept this. Accept *us*."

Eli pulled Dorran close again. He buried his face against Dorran's neck, and Dorran relaxed against him.

"I don't know what I did to earn you," Eli murmured.

"Same."

Eli snorted. "Come on. We both know I'm a stubborn asshole."

"I'm not going to deny that. It doesn't change the fact that I love you and that I don't want to lose you."

"You won't."

Dorran prayed that was the truth.

CHAPTER SEVENTEEN

Dorran had done it. He'd contacted Crawford's lawyer, and he'd told him what he had on Crawford. It hadn't been a pleasant phone call, and its result was even less pleasant since he was about to meet Crawford.

Dorran didn't want to meet the guy. He didn't even want to be in the same building as him. He wanted to stay as far away from him as possible, and possibly for Crawford to die, too. But Crawford had demanded a meeting, and Dorran didn't know how to get out of it, so he'd agreed.

At least he'd have Emanuel with him. He'd forbidden Dorran to go on his own, and even though Dorran knew how scared and nervous he was, he was there. He didn't want to face his father. He would have avoided it if he could have. But he was coming because he was Dorran's friend and he didn't want Dorran to be hurt.

Dorran hoped neither of them would be hurt.

"I don't like this," Emanuel muttered as they rode the elevator up to his father's office.

"You've been saying that since we left home."

"That's because I *really* don't like this. We shouldn't be here. You shouldn't be waving the red flag in front of the bull."

"It's going to be fine."

"Fine? Dorran, you're going to blackmail my father. *Nothing* is going to be fine."

What Emanuel didn't know was that Dorran had a plan. Dorran hoped it would be enough to get both of them out of that office in one piece, but he couldn't be sure. He had some leverage, though, and he was going to use it.

Francis had gotten him even more details, and he had a pretty good idea of the empire Crawford was at the head of. He also knew how frustrated the police department was. They'd never been able to link Crawford to any of the crimes he was so obviously guilty of. But now, thanks to Francis, Dorran *had* some proof, or at least he thought so. He wasn't sure how useful all the stuff he knew would be to the police, but he wouldn't hesitate to hand everything over once he was sure Emanuel was safe. He was still waiting for Francis to get back to him about a few things, and he'd dug out enough details in the news and on the internet to be almost a hundred percent sure that the police could finish putting things together. In the meantime, he'd make sure Emanuel was okay.

He hadn't told Eli anything. He knew better than to think that Eli wouldn't lock him in his apartment if he did. He'd have made sure Dorran wouldn't get anywhere near Crawford. Dorran felt guilty about doing this without him because he knew how freaked out Eli would be if he knew, but he couldn't think about that, not when the elevator was slowing down, about to stop on the floor they needed to get off at.

"Don't show him you're afraid," Emanuel muttered. He was wearing a suit, and it looked odd on him. "Don't show him any kind of emotion. He'll latch onto it, and that's the last thing we want."

Dorran could do that.

He thought so, anyway.

Emanuel strode out of the elevator. Dorran followed him, impressed at the way Emanuel behaved. He was so used to his friend being a flighty artist that he didn't recognize the strong, confident man.

Emanuel passed by a desk occupied by a blonde woman. She half rose from her chair and called after him, but he ignored her and pushed open the door he'd been aiming for. Dorran gave the secretary an apologetic smile and walked into Crawford's office right after Emanuel.

"I thought I'd raised you better than this," Crawford said.

Dorran wasn't sure what he'd imagined he would find, but he wasn't surprised by anything he was seeing. Crawford didn't look one bit like Emanuel, thank God. He wore his hair short. His jaw was clean shaven, but he had a neat mustache that Dorran could all too easily imagine him twirling while he laughed evilly, maybe with a long-haired cat in his lap.

"Yeah, well. You weren't exactly the best father. You know, what with killing my boyfriend and whatnot."

Crawford arched a brow. "How many times will I have to tell you I had nothing to do with that?"

"I won't ever believe you."

"I just took advantage of the situation." His gaze moved to Dorran. "So this is the man trying to blackmail me."

Dorran felt very much like a mouse standing in front of a snake. He swallowed and did his best to look like he wasn't afraid, but in truth, he was petrified. "I wouldn't call what I'm doing blackmail."

"No? What would you call it, then?"

"Insurance. I want you to leave Emanuel alone. That's it."

Crawford leaned forward. "Are you and my son lovers?"

"No. But he's my friend."

"How did you find out about all the things you told my lawyer, Mr. Wells?"

"I'm not about to tell you that." Not that he'd believe Dorran even if Dorran did. "Besides, you don't need to know. What you *do* need to know is that I won't hesitate to hand everything over to the police if you ever contact Emanuel again."

"You don't have hard proof."

Not yet, but Crawford didn't need to know that. "Are you

sure of that?"

There was a pause, and Dorran held his breath. He was mostly bluffing. Francis might have given him what he needed, but Crawford was right—he didn't have any solid proof. What he did have would help the police, hopefully, but this wasn't what this was about.

This was about convincing Crawford that if he didn't leave Emanuel alone, he'd be done for.

"I want all the copies of whatever you have," Crawford said.

Dorran fucking hoped that meant he was giving in. "I don't think so. What will stop you from threatening Emanuel again once you have them? I won't use what I have against you. I wouldn't know where to start to do that, and I'm sure you're aware of that." Dorran didn't doubt that Crawford had had someone look into him after he'd called the lawyer.

"What do I get out of this, then?"

"You get that you can continue to do your business," Emanuel snapped. "I don't want anything to do with you, ever again. In exchange for that, Dorran won't give what he has on you to the cops or the media. That will have to be enough for you."

He turned around and strode away. Dorran wasn't about to stay on his own with Crawford, so he quickly followed, trying to keep his back straight.

Emanuel only relaxed once they were back in the elevator. He slumped against the wall and loosened his tie. "Shit. That was terrifying."

"I can't imagine what growing up with him was like."

"Trust me, it's best you don't."

"Do you think he'll accept."

"Yeah. But you need to give Eli everything you have as soon as possible."

Dorran blinked. "I told you I would."

Emanuel smiled. "I know. You wouldn't let my father get away with what he did, not if you had anything to say about it. I figure you're waiting for something and that once you have it, you'll hand off everything."

"And you don't think I'm doing the wrong thing." Because no matter what, Crawford was Emanuel's father.

"As long as my father spends the rest of his life in jail, no."

Dorran hesitated. "He said he didn't have Axel killed."

"And you believe him? He's never been honest in his life, Dorran. He's not going to start now."

Dorran wasn't so sure of that, but he didn't push. Still, why wouldn't Crawford admit to killing Axel? It wasn't like Dorran didn't know he'd killed other people. He'd sent the files he'd gathered to Stone, and he had no doubt Stone had shared them with his client. Denying he'd killed Axel made no sense, but then, Dorran didn't know Crawford, and he didn't want to know him, either. He was just glad he and Emanuel had made it out alive and in one piece.

"How did you get all that info anyway?" Emanuel asked, his voice quiet.

Dorran hesitated. "I want to tell you."

"But you'd have to kill me if you did?"

"No. I just don't think now is the right moment. You've already been through enough in such a short time."

"You're not wrong. You'll tell me once this mess is over?"

"As long as everyone involved is okay with it."

Emanuel grimaced. "I was afraid you'd say someone else was involved."

"Don't worry about him. Your father can't do anything to him."

"I hope you're right, Dorran."

Dorran was only sure of one thing in his life right now, and it was that Francis would be okay.

It wasn't like he could be killed a second time, right?

CHAPTER EIGHTEEN

Dorran's phone chirped while he was in the shower. He almost smashed his head against the tiles in his haste to grab it from the sink where he'd left it, and of course, he dropped it to the floor. "Damn it."

It had better not be his mother or one of his siblings, not when he was waiting for Crawford's lawyer to contact him and tell him what Crawford was planning to do. Whatever he chose, Dorran would be handing over everything Francis had gathered to the police, but the haste in which he'd do it would be different. He'd have slightly more time if Crawford agreed to his request of leaving Emanuel alone, but even if he did, Dorran doubted it would be for long. The man was lethal, and he wouldn't hesitate to kill Dorran if it made his life easier. The only thing that was saving Dorran, for now, was probably the fact that Crawford didn't know who else had a copy of what he knew.

Yet.

The phone chirped again. Dorran grabbed a towel and dried his hand and face. Then he reached over the tub. His fingertips brushed against his phone, but it was just slightly out of reach, and Dorran still needed to rinse.

He huffed and went to work. He did a quick job of getting the soap off his body. He left his conditioner in his hair—it always looked better when he did—and turned the water off. He toweled just enough not to drip all over the bathroom floor, then he hopped out of the tub—and nearly crashed against the wall when he got tangled in the shower curtain.

He was still glaring at it when he reached down to grab his phone.

My father agreed to your terms! Emanuel had texted.

Dorran leaned against the tiled wall, hissed at the coolness of it, and moved forward again. He was so fucking relieved he could have started singing. The main reason he didn't was that he thought Francis was somewhere in the apartment and he'd tease him endlessly since he couldn't sing to save his life.

He scrolled down to read the second text he'd gotten, still from Emanuel.

He told me I was dead to him, which isn't a bad thing since I'm still breathing.

Dorran frowned. He knew how much Emanuel disliked his father, and he was no doubt relieved at not having to deal with the man ever again, but it wasn't fair. Of course, there was little that was fair in this situation, and Dorran supposed that as long as he was safe, Emanuel would be more than happy to stay as far away as he could from his father. He'd probably be *happy* never to see him again. Dorran knew he would be. Crawford had given him the creeps, and he'd only met him for about five minutes. He couldn't imagine what life for Emanuel had been like growing up with him.

So, want to celebrate? Emanuel's next text said.

Dorran decided to call him. "What did you have in mind?" he asked when Emanuel answered.

"I don't know. Nothing extreme since I have to stand on my own two feet from now on."

"So it's not a celebration."

"Fuck yes, it is. I'm finally free from my father, and it's worth having to pay my own bills. I should have broken contact with him a long time ago. Axel might not be dead right now if I had."

Emanuel still seemed to be convinced that his father had had Axel killed. Dorran wasn't sure what to think at this point. He wouldn't trust Crawford with a used coffee capsule, but why would the man have lied when Emanuel had asked him if he'd killed his boyfriend? At that point, the three of them had known he was responsible for more than a few deaths. Lying didn't make much sense, not when Crawford didn't seem to regret anything he'd done. Hell, Dorran suspected he would have crowed about killing Axel because it would have hurt Emanuel.

But Crawford wasn't his father, and Emanuel knew him better than Dorran ever would, thank God.

"I doubt anything you could have done would have changed what happened to Axel."

Emanuel sighed. "Maybe. But let's not talk about this, yeah? I want to celebrate being a free man. Maybe we can go to the bar down the street? Have a beer or two and talk about your love life problems?"

Dorran groaned. "We can get a drink, but only if you don't mention Eli or my love life in any way, shape, or form."

"That bad?"

"Actually, no. We've pretty much made peace, even though things aren't perfect yet."

"Things will never be perfect, Dorran. As long as you and Eli love each other and are ready to work together to make both of you happy, then I don't see what the problem is. You're not dating Eli's mother."

Dorran shuddered at the thought. "When are we meeting?" he asked, not willing to think about dating Eli's mother.

"When can you be ready?"

"Isn't it a little early to drink?"

"It's beer time somewhere. Come on, Dorran. I want to get drunk on the thought that my father is out of my life for good."

Dorran laughed. "And on beer."

"And on beer."

"I guess we can meet in half an hour. Is that soon enough

for you?"

"I'll make do."

Dorran rolled his eyes. He might have some reservations about Crawford being behind Axel's death, and he might be terrified at the thought of what Crawford would eventually do—there was no way the man would let Dorran blackmail him for long, not when he'd killed people for less—but for now, Dorran would relax. He hadn't heard Emanuel being this relaxed and giddy in, well, ever, and his neighbor deserved to be able to stop worrying about his father and his dead boyfriend for an evening. All of that would still be there tomorrow when he woke up, and he'd also have to start dealing with the fact that his father wouldn't send him money anymore.

But he was free from his father, and apparently, he was more than a little happy about that.

Francis was lounging on the couch when Dorran finally left his bedroom after getting dressed. He arched a brow when Dorran put his shoes on. "Where are you going? Seeing Eli?"

"No. Emanuel wants to celebrate."

"Celebrate what? He just lost his boyfriend."

"And he's finally free from his father. Besides, you know he and Axel weren't in love."

Francis tsked. "Still. As far as I know, that investigation is still ongoing. It's not going to look good for him to celebrate mere days after his boyfriend was stabbed to death."

"I'll make sure he doesn't drink too much."

Francis nodded and got up. "I'll try to find Axel again and see if he's getting better at this being dead thing. Maybe he can finally tell me who stabbed him."

"Maybe." Dorran hoped he would, because he didn't have Emanuel's certainty when it came to his father's guilt. He wanted to see the real killer behind bars, as well as Emanuel's father. "Thanks."

Francis blinked. "What for?"

"For helping. I know life would be easier for you if you could just, I don't know, haunt the apartment all day."

"Dorran, life can't get easier for me. I'm *dead*, remember?"

"You won't let me forget it, so yes, I do."

Francis rolled his eyes and faded away. Dorran waited until he was gone to chuckle and get to the front door. Living with a ghost had a learning curve, but Dorran loved it.

He would probably have loved sharing the apartment with a living Francis, too, but Dorran was glad to see that Francis wasn't letting death stop him. He was dead, but he was still there, and he was still taking care of the people he considered family, like Emanuel. Dorran didn't know what would happen next, but he knew he wouldn't renounce this new, weird, ability of his even if he could have—which he didn't. Carole had been clear about that.

Dorran was going to have to learn to live with it, and so would Eli if he was going to stick around.

Dorran wasn't drunk, even though Emanuel had done his best to change that. He hadn't stopped at three beers like Dorran had, and he was stumbling ahead of Dorran as they walked home. Dorran supposed he should be grateful neither of them needed to drive tonight. He might not be drunk, but he wouldn't have trusted himself behind the wheel.

"What am I going to do now?" Emanuel moaned. He almost fell on his face, but Dorran managed to grab the back of his shirt and hold him upright.

So *this* was why Emanuel had drunk so much. "You're going to go to bed and feel like shit tomorrow morning when you wake up."

Emanuel's head rolled toward Dorran. "I know that. I meant once I have to pay my bills."

"You'll sell a few more paintings than you usually do.

Everything will be fine, Emanuel. You were the one who told me you'd manage."

"What if I can't?"

"Then you'll find yourself another job. There's no shame in that, and while I understand you'd rather spend your days painting, you'll do what you have to do. And if you have trouble, I'll help." Dorran wouldn't be able to do much, but he'd certainly try.

Emanuel grinned and looped an arm around Dorran's shoulders. "I like you. You know, if you weren't with that man of yours, I might have tried to lure you into my bed."

Dorran was pretty sure Emanuel wouldn't have said that if he hadn't been drunk. "I don't think you're my type, but I'll take it as a compliment."

"It was. And I'm *everyone's* type, Dorran."

"If you say so." It was amusing to see Emanuel this way. He was usually much more controlled, except when he painted. Then he forgot the rest of the world and focused on the white surface in front of him.

Dorran managed to herd Emanuel into his apartment—he had to grab the keys from Emanuel's pocket, and Emanuel wiggled his eyebrows at him in what he probably thought was a come-hither gesture. It looked more like he was having a stroke, but Dorran didn't say anything. He dragged Emanuel to his bedroom, dumped him onto the bed, and by the time he was back from the kitchen with a bottle of water and aspirin, Emanuel was already asleep.

"He's going to regret drinking tomorrow," Dorran muttered as he put the water and the painkillers onto the nightstand. At least Emanuel would have them close when he came back to the reality.

Dorran took Emanuel's shoes off, but that was where he drew the line even though sleeping in jeans was so damn uncomfortable. When he left, Emanuel was snoring softly, unaware of his surroundings.

Dorran rubbed his face as he closed Emanuel's door and walked down the short path to his own apartment. He was tired, and his eyes burned, and he couldn't wait to get to bed even though it wasn't that late. He and Emanuel had gone to the bar early, and it hadn't taken much for Emanuel to get drunk, not with the way he'd been drinking down beers before moving on to tequila. It was just after ten PM now, and Dorran was looking forward to a long night of sleep.

He frowned when he went to unlock his front door only to find it open. He didn't remember leaving it unlocked when he'd left, but then, he also didn't remember locking it. He wasn't surprised he'd forgotten, not when Emanuel had been impatient and pulling at his arms so they'd get to the bar faster.

Dorran smiled and shook his head. Emanuel was scared, but he'd be fine. Dorran was sure of that.

He pushed his front door open and stepped in. Francis appeared in front of him, his eyes wide. He yelled, "Duck!" and Dorran obeyed without thinking twice about it.

Something whooshed past Dorran's head. He didn't know what it was, but he didn't waste time finding out. He threw himself to the side and twisted to face whoever was attacking him.

What the fuck was it with killers trying to get even with him when he hadn't done anything? Okay, maybe that wasn't quite right. He couldn't deny he'd stuck his nose into too many investigations, but still. That didn't mean people had to try to fucking kill him.

The man attacking him—it was dark, but Dorran was pretty sure it was Mr. Warren—swung at Dorran again. Dorran had no idea what he was trying to hit him with, and he wasn't sure he wanted to find out. As long as it wasn't a knife, he could probably stay out of the man's path and manage to get back out the door.

Probably.

"What can I do?" Francis asked. He tried to touch Mr. Warren, but of course, his hand just went right through the man.

"Go get someone," Dorran hissed. He noticed Warren look around, no doubt to find out who he was talking to.

Dorran tried to take advantage of that and rushed toward the door, but Warren kicked it, slamming it shut. Dorran hoped someone had heard that and would come to complain, but he didn't want to put his faith in that, not when Emanuel was out like a light, and the other neighbors tended to keep to themselves.

"Who?" Francis asked.

"How the fuck should I know?" And how the fuck was he supposed to leave the apartment when Warren was standing in front of the door?

Dorran licked his lips and raised his hands. "Okay. Look, I don't know why you're here—"

"To help my daughter."

Okay, that made sense. "Your daughter?" Maybe if Dorran got Warren to talk, Francis would have enough time to go grab someone. Dorran didn't even care who at this point, as long as Warren stopped trying to hit him with a hammer.

Jesus.

Warren pointed the hammer at Dorran. It looked heavy, and Dorran could too easily imagine what it would have felt like as it shattered his head. "You said there was a print on the knife."

Dorran blinked. He *had* said that when he'd last talked to Warren, but he wasn't sure what it had to do with him. "The *police* have the knife and the print. Even if you kill me, they won't stop investigating." And he looked like he just might. "They're going to find out who the print belongs to even if I'm not there. I mean, I don't have anything to do with the investigation."

"You came to talk to Maggie and me."

"Because the police had arrested one of my friends for Axel's murder and I knew he hadn't done it. I was trying to find clues. I didn't find the print, and even if I had, I wouldn't have been able to do anything about it. I'm not a cop." But he knew one, and since it looked like either Warren or his daughter had killed Axel, he was going to make sure Eli knew about it.

That was, if he made it out alive. That hammer was scary, especially if he thought about what Warren was planning to do with it.

Warren didn't seem to care about what Dorran had just told him. He swung the hammer upward, and Dorran just had time to get out of the way. It still hit him, and it fucking hurt, but it could have been much worse.

Maybe Dorran could run to his bedroom and lock himself in there until someone arrived. Francis was finally gone, and Dorran prayed that meant he *was* getting help and not that he'd decided he wanted a ghostly roommate.

Dorran scrambled toward the bedroom, Warren at his heels. He felt the hammer almost touching him a few times, and he knew it was a miracle that it hadn't—and that his luck wouldn't last long. Warren might not be a good killer, but there was no doubt in Dorran's mind that he wasn't going to stop trying until Dorran was bloody and not breathing anymore.

Dorran slammed against the wall. He rolled to the side, and Warren's hammer went straight through the plywood. A small cloud of dust puffed out. Warren managed to wrangle the hammer out of the wall, and Dorran didn't hang around to see what would happen next. His arm hurt, and he hoped it wasn't broken, although if he died, it wouldn't make much of a difference.

He'd take the pain over death any day, though.

CHAPTER NINETEEN

W arren raised his hammer again.
  The front door burst open, the hallway light streaming into the dark apartment. "Drop your weapon!" someone yelled.

Dorran sobbed when he recognized Eli's voice, but he knew better than to stop or even try to get to Eli. Instead, he dove for the bedroom door.

He'd left it open, and with Warren distracted, he managed to barrel into the bedroom and slam the door shut. He pressed his back against it even though he realized it probably wasn't the smartest idea. His arm was pulsing, and when he gently touched it, he hissed at the pain. His hand came back wet, with blood, probably. Dorran wasn't about to move from where he was until he was sure the coast was clear, though.

He expected to hear a shot, but it looked like Warren was smarter than Dorran had thought.

"Put that hammer down, Warren. It's over."

"I wasn't doing anything."

Dorran almost snorted, but he didn't want to get Warren's attention, not when he was so close to the bedroom door.

"You're in my boyfriend's apartment, threatening him with a hammer. And that hole in the wall doesn't speak of home renovations. Put the hammer down before I decide to shoot your ass for terrifying Dorran."

"You can't do that."

"Trust me, I don't care that much about what I can and can't do, not when it comes to my boyfriend."

The heavy thump Dorran heard made it easier to breathe, even though he couldn't be sure Warren had dropped the hammer.

Dorran listened to Eli arresting Warren and reading him his rights. Dorran knew Eli wouldn't come to him until he was sure Warren wasn't a danger anymore, but he was stunned when he heard more people entering his apartment.

"I caught him in flagrant—" Eli said.

Dorran couldn't hear everything, and he was pretty sure it was safe to open the door now. It wasn't even locked, so it probably wouldn't have been that good of a shield. It might have slowed Warren down, but that was about it.

The door creaked when it opened. Eli was talking to a woman in uniform, but his head snapped up at the sound. His expression relaxed, and he rushed toward Dorran, leaving the cop behind. "Dorran."

Dorran jerked back when Eli touched his hurt arm. Eli's eyes widened, and he barked, "Call an ambulance."

"I don't need an ambulance," Dorran protested. He didn't *think* he needed one anyway. His arm worked, even though it hurt, and it was bleeding.

"Your arm."

"I'll be fine. I just need it cleaned." And maybe some painkillers, although since he'd drunk tonight, that wasn't the smartest idea. He was entirely sober now, but he didn't want to risk it.

Eli wrapped his arm around Dorran's shoulders and pulled him close, careful of Dorran's arm in a way that made Dorran's chest tighten. "I was so scared I was going to lose you," Eli murmured.

"Where's Warren?"

"I called Mel on my way here. He took care of Warren and called reinforcements in."

Dorran frowned. "On your way here?"

"Yes. Carole called me."

"*Carole* called you?"

Eli nodded. "I'll tell you later, okay?"

Dorran took that as meaning ghosts were involved, and Eli didn't want to talk about it in front of other cops. That was fine with Dorran. He wanted to be alone with Eli to mope for a bit.

Dorran had to answer a whole lot of questions, ignore Eli's glare when he explained he'd visited Maggie Ford and her father to ask them about Axel's death and let the paramedics patch him up. He didn't go to the hospital, though. There was no need for him to, not when the paramedics agreed with him that the hammer only grazed him and that nothing was broken. Unfortunately, the paramedics also agreed that Dorran should wait a bit longer before taking painkillers, and Dorran knew Eli would make sure he didn't get them too soon.

Dorran would have grumbled if Eli hadn't bundled him up and settled on the couch while he saw the paramedics and the lingering police officers out. Dorran heard him promise to call Mel first thing in the morning before closing the door.

That was when Dorran opened his eyes. He watched Eli pace the length of the living room a few times. Eli looked like he'd been through the wringer—his hair stood up as if he'd raked his hands through it one too many times, his tie was crooked, and blue shadows were forming under his eyes.

"Sit down with me?" Dorran asked after a few moments.

"Of course." Eli took off his tie and his jacket, toed off his shoes, and settled next to Dorran under the blanket he'd wrapped Dorran in. Dorran snuggled close to him and sighed, closing his eyes again.

He was home. What had happened didn't matter, not anymore.

"How did Carole call you?"

"Ah. I was wondering if you'd forgotten I'd said that."

"Of course I didn't. I know how much you hate Carole."

Eli sighed. "I don't hate her. I don't even dislike her. I don't know her well enough to. I just don't like what her presence in your life means."

Dorran patted Eli's chest. "I know, and trust me, I'd be perfectly happy without the seeing ghosts shit if I could. But the thing is, I can't. For whatever reason, I have this ability, and that's not going to change. I could try ignoring it, but Carole knows what she's talking about when she says it would make my life hell. I'm working on blocking the ghosts I don't want around and on calling on the ones I do want to talk to. It doesn't mean I have to do anything more than making sure my life isn't taken over by ghosts, though. I'm not going into the business of being a psychic like she is, don't worry. I just want control." Dorran smiled. "And don't think I haven't noticed you didn't tell me why she called you."

"I didn't recognize her number, and thank God for that because I doubt I would have answered if I had. She told me Axel's ghost had been hanging around his ex-wife and her kids. Her father came to talk to her, and Axel heard that she'd been the one who'd killed him. He remembered a lot once he found that out apparently, but that wasn't why Carole called. She said Axel heard that Warren was going to come here and make sure you couldn't stick your nose into the investigation again. I guess he wanted to protect his daughter. So Axel found Carole because it seems that she's stronger than you or something like that, and she called me." He kissed the top of Dorran's head. "Francis also found me, by the way. I was already on my way here when he appeared out of nowhere to tell me a mad man with a hammer was attacking you. I don't think I've ever been so scared in my life."

"Mmm, I don't know about that. How about when I was shot?"

Eli gently pinched Dorran's side. "Shut up. You're not making this any easier."

"Sorry." Dorran relaxed even more. "I'm tired."

"You can go to sleep. I'll be here making sure no one else tries to shoot you or hammer your brain in."

"Of course you will."

Dorran was almost asleep when Eli next spoke. "And I'm going to tell my parents about you."

Dorran had a hard time waking himself up enough to answer. "You don't have to do that."

"Yeah, I do, and it's not because *you* want me to. I can't stop thinking about what my life would have been like if Warren had succeeded. I wouldn't have been able to lean on my family while I grieved you, and while I never want to think about you dying again, I can't ignore that keeping you away from them is doing a lot more bad than good. I know my mom especially won't take it easily, but it's time. I want you to come to Sunday lunches with me, Dorran, and to sit by my side when we go."

EPILOGUE

Dorran hadn't expected Eli to be so literal when he'd said he wanted him by his side at Sunday lunch. He certainly hadn't expected it to happen on the next Sunday.

He looked at the house where Eli had parked. They were on the street because the driveway was already occupied. "Are you sure about this? I mean, you only told them a few days ago." Dorran had been attacked on Sunday, and Eli hadn't left his side until Wednesday. Once he had, he'd gone straight to his parents and had told them he was still very much gay and in a relationship with Dorran.

Dorran had no idea how things had gone. The only thing he'd managed to get out of Eli was that things had gone *fine*, but that wasn't very telling. What did fine mean? That his mother hadn't fainted when she'd heard the news? Or that she'd accepted that Eli was with Dorran and that she was already planning their wedding? Dorran wouldn't be surprised if she was, knowing her, but he doubted things had gone that easily, not when Eli had been terrified of telling her even last week

"And I also told them you'd be coming with me today."

"That doesn't mean it's a good idea. I doubt your mom is over the moon about this." Dorran cleared his throat. "Have you heard about what's going to happen to Warren?"

Eli arched a brow. He had to know Dorran was trying to waste time, but that was okay with Dorran as long as he answered. He wasn't fooling himself into thinking Eli would drive him home. He was there now, and there would be no going back. He could complain as much as he wanted to, but Eli wouldn't let him get out of it, and he wasn't wrong. Dorran had wanted this to happen. He couldn't deny it was intimidating, though.

He remembered Eli's family and their house, and while they'd always been nice to him, this wasn't the same thing. They'd never known that Eli and Dorran were in love, or that they were together.

"He's still in jail."

Dorran brought his attention back to Eli. "Because he got into my apartment?"

"That and because of what he did. He helped his daughter hide the fact that she'd killed her ex-husband, and he tried to frame Emanuel."

"How did he get into Emanuel's apartment?" And in Dorran's because now Dorran was sure he'd locked his door when he'd left.

"He has a past of breaking and entering."

"And you didn't know about it?"

Eli frowned. "Of course I did. We found that out the day after Axel was killed. Breaking and entering isn't murder, though, and Warren had never been accused of anything violent."

"Until now."

"Until now. He wanted to make sure his daughter wouldn't be accused of murder."

"But she did kill Axel. Right?"

"Yeah." Eli sighed. "She's not talking anymore, but when we arrested her, she did. It looks like she went to Axel's house because he was going to push for a divorce. He told her he was in love with Emanuel and that he wanted to start a new life with him."

"He didn't know Emanuel didn't feel the same way."

"It doesn't look like it, no."

Maybe it wasn't a bad thing. Axel had died thinking he was loved, and there were worst things in the world — like being stabbed to death by your ex-wife and the mother of your children. "What about the kids?"

"They're with Axel's parents right now."

Dorran felt sorry for them. They'd lost both their parents and one of their grandparents. He hoped they'd be okay. He didn't know for sure, since he hadn't talked to Axel again, but he suspected that was why Axel had lied to him. Even though his ex-wife had killed him, he hadn't wanted their kids to lose both their parents. "What about that other stuff I gave you?" Dorran had dumped the files he'd gathered on Crawford in Eli's hands as soon as he'd woken up the day after Warren had attacked him. He hoped Crawford wasn't about to come after him, but he wouldn't take the chance.

"Mel and I are still going over it, but we're probably going to have to hand it off. How did you find out all that stuff, Dorran?"

"Francis. He stayed with Crawford for a bit."

Eli grimaced. "Yeah, I'm not going to be able to give that explanation. I'll just say I found it on my desk one morning or something."

"Thank you. I don't want to be involved." He'd had enough with everything that had happened. Warren had insisted he hadn't broken into Dorran's apartment that first time, and Dorran was inclined to believe him. He suspected Emanuel's father had tried to keep him away from his son, maybe to make sure Emanuel would go home. He had no proof, and he had no intention of looking for it. He was done with this.

"I don't want you to be, either. You always end up hurt when you are." He cleared his throat. "Ready to go?"

Dorran wasn't, but he nodded anyway. He doubted he'd ever be ready to go and meet Eli's family as his boyfriend, but he was about to anyway.

They left the car, and Dorran's eyes widened when Eli grabbed his hand. He didn't let go, using his hold to drag Dorran to the front door while quickly knocking with his free hand. He didn't wait for someone to come open. Instead, he pushed open the door. "Mom?" he yelled out.

The scents in the air were divine. Dorran recognized garlic, oregano, tomato sauce, and more. He doubted they'd be having pizza, but he hoped for pasta. He remembered what a good cook Eli's mother was, and it had been so long since he'd had a satisfying home-made meal. The stuff he cooked didn't count, since he never took a lot of time. He cooked just enough to eat because he hated being in the kitchen.

"She's in the kitchen," Eli said.

Dorran swallowed. He could do this. He already knew Eli's family, even though he hadn't seen them in so long. He'd be fine, and hopefully, so would everyone else.

Eli's mother *was* in the kitchen — Dorran could hear her banging pots and pans — but the rest of his family was in the living room. His father was sitting in the same armchair he'd used the first time Dorran had come around, with the TV on. No one was watching it, though.

Eli's brothers were here, and damn if they hadn't changed. Dorran remembered them as little more than teenagers, even though Julian was four years older than Eli. He was there with his wife, Andrea, but Dorran didn't know her yet. Austin was one year younger than Dorran, and he was there alone.

They were all talking and laughing, but they stopped when Eli pulled Dorran into the room. Eli behaved as if he didn't notice, smiling and saying hello. "You guys remember Dorran, right?" he said.

His father got up. Norman Hayes had been a police officer before he retired after getting shot. He still limped, but that wasn't what Dorran noticed. No, what Dorran saw was the smile on his face—a smile he hadn't expected.

"Dorran! It's been so long," Norman said.

Dorran wasn't surprised to be pulled into a hug—Eli's mother might be the Italian of the family, but they were all touchy-feely, including Eli, although in his case it was only when he knew the people he was with.

He patted Norman's back. "Well, I only met Eli again a few months ago."

Norman leaned back and grinned. "I've heard all about that."

"Not *all* of it, I hope." Dorran snapped his mouth shut, but it was too late.

Norman blinked. His smile slipped a bit, but it formed again. "I have to say, this isn't what I imagined when Eli told us he was gay."

"What did you imagine, Dad?" Eli asked. "Wait, let me guess. That I'd start dressing like one of those drag queens in the show Andrea likes to watch?"

Norman laughed. "I should have known better. You're not going to change, no matter who you're in love with. Your mother is waiting for you in the kitchen. You should go say hello."

This was what Dorran was afraid of. It looked like the rest of Eli's family was accepting, but what about his mother? He supposed he was about to find out.

Eli didn't let Dorran's hand go when they walked to the kitchen, even though Dorran could tell he was nervous.

"Mom?"

She was facing the stove, but she turned when she heard Eli's voice. Her gaze went straight to Dorran as she cleaned her hands on a tea towel. "Eli. It's about time. You're late."

Eli chuckled. "Sorry. I told you Dorran was hurt."

"I'm not hurt," Dorran protested. His arm ached a bit still, but it was nothing terrible. No, the reason they were late was that they'd spent too much time making out on Dorran's couch.

Vera, Eli's mother, tsked. "Eli told us about that mad man with the hammer. Do you want me to check your arm, Dorran?"

Dorran blinked. "No, I'm fine." He hadn't expected that. Vera hadn't hugged him, but she also wasn't kicking him out, and she genuinely sounded worried about him.

"Good. Then you and Eli can help me get everything to the dining room. Come on, boys. Get to work."

Dorran knew what this was even without being told.

She was accepting him in her family. He wouldn't have been asked to help if she wasn't, because guests didn't help, they sat down and let the family do their stuff. It was still an uneasy truce, but it *was* a truce, and Dorran didn't doubt that Vera would eventually fully accept him as Eli's boyfriend. He was surprised — and relieved.

Maybe this wasn't going to be a disaster after all.

You may also enjoy the following from eXtasy Books Inc:

Lee
Catherine Lievens

Excerpt

"It's gonna fall."

"No, it's not."

"I'm telling you, you're going to drop it, and then Lee won't want to talk to us ever again."

Lee rolled his eyes—damn brothers! "I already don't want to talk to you ever again. Why do you think I'm moving out?"

Lee had to admit he was slightly worried for the stuff Jamie was carrying. He'd decided it would be a good idea to balance a lamp on top of the two boxes he was holding, and Lee could too easily imagine the lamp shattering on the floor. He wouldn't care much, but their mom would, since she'd been the one who'd selected and bought it.

Jamie snorted. "We're just as relieved to see you go, asshole."

"Aww. Won't you miss my pretty face in the morning?"

"I'll miss having Brandon around more."

"We all miss him," Miles said as he snatched the lamp.

Lee breathed more easily. "He's not dead, you know," he

pointed out.

"He might as well be. He's mated."

"Not yet. Well, he and Maddox aren't bonded yet." Although Lee wasn't sure if that was because they'd decided to wait or because of the circumstances. He didn't think he'd want to bond, not after they'd lost Nathalie, but he wasn't Brandon.

God, just the thought of her and what she'd done made Lee so angry. And how had he not seen what was happening with her? He and Brandon had talked about it, and Brandon felt the same way. Lee thought Brandon had extenuating circumstances—a guy had drugged him and tried to rape him, then to kill him. And in the middle of that, he'd met his mate and moved in with him. And he was only nineteen.

Brandon made Lee feel like he needed to get his life under control, which was one of the reasons he was moving into his new apartment in Gillham, not far from the animal shelter where he and Brandon had summer jobs. Lee suspected Brandon would spend more time hanging from Maddox's lips than working, but then, he was probably going to coo over every single animal and try to take them home. Not that he had the space to do that, but maybe he could get a cat or something. Or he could go over to Maddox and Brandon's house and cuddle their pets. They had what felt like a dozen of them.

Miles waved. "They're going to do it sooner or later."

Lee arched a brow. "Do it? I didn't know you thought about them that way."

Miles' cheeks flushed. "That's disgusting. Brandon's like my brother. Hell, I like him more than I like you, and we are brothers."

Lee had been adopted, and having Jamie and Miles treat him like they were actually related always thrilled him. "That's because you don't understand the splendor that I am."

"Yeah, right. So, where do I put this?" He held up the lamp.

Lee looked around the apartment. It was furnished, thanks

to Kameron and the pack, but Lee's personal stuff was still in the boxes he and his brothers had been carrying up the stairs for what felt like an eternity. "I have no idea."

"I'd personally put it into the trashcan," Jamie said. He dumped the two boxes he'd been holding onto a growing pile of other boxes. "That thing is ugly. Does Mom think we're still in the sixties? Lava lamps haven't been in since about then."

Lee shrugged. "I like it." He wasn't crazy about it, but he doubted he'd have a lot of visitors who'd see it, and the people who would come around knew his mom and wouldn't be surprised.

Miles pointed the lamp at Lee. "You're never going to find yourself a husband with this thing in your apartment."

"I don't want a husband."

"A boyfriend, then."

"I'm sure whoever I end up with will love the lamp." Lee didn't think he'd find someone anytime soon, though. He wanted some time to get used to this new life of his—a new apartment, one of his best friends in a serious relationship with their mate, the other one behind bars after betraying them for drugs. Sometimes, Lee wondered if he shouldn't have stayed home, where everything was familiar. He knew what to expect then, but he had no idea what tomorrow would bring him here.

"Lee?"

Brandon! Lee grinned, and Brandon appeared at the door a few seconds later, carrying four pizza boxes. Maddox was right behind him with two bags containing bottles, probably water and soda, since Lee hadn't yet gone grocery shopping. That was something he'd have to remember to do now, and he wasn't looking forward to it.

"Sorry we're late," Brandon said. He held up the boxes. "But we brought an apology."

"We should fight every day, if this is the kind of apologies you give," Jamie said. He made grabby hands, and Brandon handed him the boxes.

"Why don't you set up at the table? I think Mom put napkins in one of the boxes." Lee wasn't sure what box exactly, so hopefully he wouldn't have to open many of them. Of course, since his brothers were helping him move, he found the box labeled kitchen stuff in his bedroom.

"How are you holding up?" Brandon asked, startling Lee.

"Holding up? You make it sound like someone died."

Brandon shrugged. "Nat didn't die, but it feels a bit like she did, doesn't it?"

"I have no right to be angry with her, not like you."

"No right? Lee, she might have only put me in the hands of that drug dealer, but that doesn't mean she didn't hurt you, too." Brandon bit his lower lip. "And I know I hurt you when I told you I wouldn't move in with you. We had these plans, and I—"

ABOUT THE AUTHOR

Catherine lives in Italy, country of good food and hot men. She used to write fantasy as a child, but it was reading her first gay erotic romance novel that made her realize that that was what she really wanted to write.

After graduating from college in English language and translation, she divides her day between writing, reading, taking care of her son and reading some more.

You can find her on Facebook and Twitter or on her website: authorcatherinelievens.wordpress.com

Email: lievens.catherine@gmail.com

Newsletter: http://eepurl.com/c-uvKn